How Not to Marry a Prince

Megan Derr

How Not to Marry a Prince
By Megan Derr

Published by Megan Derr

Edited by Samantha M. Derr
Cover designed by Aisha Akeju

First Edition August 2022

Printed in the United States of America

Dedicated In Loving Memory to

Elena Nicole Allen

Who never got to be
But was loved all the same

Goodnight, Moonlight Lady

Arrival

True to form for the joke that his life had become, Amador arrived in the kingdom of Portan amidst a thunderstorm, looking very much like a soaked cat and at least twice as cranky about it.

Still better than the time he'd arrived covered in mud with a twisted ankle, thanks to a bad combination of pigs, farm boys, and beer. But not by much.

He waved off the servants who came rushing to help him, not wanting them to get soaked as well, and trudged up the stairs until he was under the relative safety of the canopy that had been erected over the entrance. Removing his glasses, he tucked them away in the front pocket of his soaked jacket. "Is this rain typical for this time of year?"

One of the nearby guards snorted, and the servants all bit back laughs and smiles. "Typical for every time of year, I'm afraid,

Your Highness. Between the mountains to the north and the lakes everywhere, we get a great deal of rain and snow, with some hail and sleet to keep it interesting."

"Intriguing," Amador replied. "Where I'm from, we're lucky to see rain twice a year. Thank you," he added as one of them offered him a large, toasty warm towel. "I've a carriage and luggage cart coming behind me, but I've no idea when it will arrive, given the weather."

"We'll be on the lookout, Your Highness," another servant said.

Still a third approached with a steaming mug on a silver tray. "Hot toddy, Your Highness?"

"I've no idea what that is, but I like the sound of 'hot' very much, thank you." Amador took a generous swallow and then wheezed. "Alcohol. Marvelous. If there is someone who can show me to my room, I will gladly take this with me and ask for another when I arrive."

The servants laughed, which improved Amador's mood immensely. He very much doubted he was actually funny, but he was very much certain these poor people dealt with jerks all day, especially in harsh weather, and were grateful simply for someone who wasn't an ass.

One of them, about ten in all, broke

away from the others, swept a beautiful bow, and escorted Amador into the palace.

Its official name was Harridor Palace. Detractors like to call it Harridan Palace. Mostly, though, it was called the Palace of a Thousand Roses, for it boasted a collection unrivaled anywhere in the world. If there was a rose that existed, and even many that were only thoughts and dreams, they could be found there, either in the public gardens, the private gardens, or the fiercely guarded greenhouses.

Thankfully, the rainy weather seemed to be keeping people shut up in their rooms, or their lovers' rooms, and Amador did not have to stop and chat a hundred times while doing his best impression of a damp cat. Unfortunately, the palace was enormous, even larger than his parents' nigh-garish home, and that meant he tracked wet footprints through the whole thing, ruining the day of at least half a dozen servants.

"Here you are, Your Highness, and dinner is served at nine, if you'd like to attend. If you prefer to remain in your rooms tonight, simply leave the appropriate card in the door slot."

"Of course, thank you so much," Amador replied, having no idea whatsoever what the woman was talking about.

Alone at last, at least until his personal

staff arrived, Amador went in search of something warm and dry to wear. It took him only moments to find the dressing room, and in it were three dressing robes, all of them in his size, each a drastically different style, along with matching slippers and even hair wraps, though his was too short to need such a thing.

At the far end of the room, directly opposite the door, was yet another door. Curious. Amador opened it, and immediately gasped in delight. A private bathing chamber. After so much traveling in places where public bathing was the rule, and even royal suites tended to share, this was a positive delight.

Stripping off his clothes and leaving them in a hamper, more than happy to let someone else deal with that problem, he ran a bath that filled the whole room with steam. Once he'd scrubbed thoroughly clean, he sank into the hot water, scented with jasmine oil, and groaned as the heat soaked into his travel-weary bones.

Of course, now that he was holding still, all his worries came crashing back to the forefront of his mind, eager to be the center of attention once more. Amador sighed.

The Palace of a Thousand Roses was his last chance. If he couldn't convince Prince Nazaire that he was the ideal spouse, that was it for him. He'd be dragged home to marry

Prince Ottokar and forced to spend the rest of his life subject to Ottakar's every vicious whim. He'd been nasty as a child, mean when they were students, and was now positively cruel as an adult. Amador had the scars to prove it, not that anybody ever bothered to ask.

He closed his eyes and took several deep breaths. The last time he'd seen Ottokar was across the ocean in Werth. There was nothing to worry about where he was concerned, except that he *had* to make this marriage work.

If only he wasn't facing a prince who had rejected each and every suitor that had shown up. Rumor had it he was an entitled brat who was impossible to please, spoiled rotten his whole life by his doting eldest brother, King Sohan. Their parents had died when Sohan was only ten, and Nazaire little more than a babe. They had two sisters between them, one who had gone off to marry Queen Penelope of Tarath, and the other was a scholar of no small acclaim. Amador had hoped to encounter her on his travels, but no such luck.

Climbing out of the bath, he dried off and looked over the tray of lotions, settling on one that had the same jasmine scent as the bath oil he'd used. He started at the bottom and worked his way up, paying special care to the still-tender scar on his arm where a piece of glass had sliced it open, and the twin surgical scars on his chest that were years old but which he was meticulous with all the same. Redolent in jasmine, he grabbed one of the dressing robes on his way back to the bedroom proper—where he was delighted to see that a fresh hot toddy was waiting for him, along with a small meal to tide him over until dinner.

Which reminded him, he needed to figure out what that servant had meant by leaving the appropriate card in the door.

Returning to the door, he examined the gold-stained console table beside it, which contained a dish to hold odds and ends, a bouquet of white roses… and, indeed, a stack of large, rectangular cards, made of good cardstock, each one an assorted color, with embossed symbols painted in white.

There were six in all: green, yellow, red, blue, purple, and black.

The black one bore a symbol of a snake wrapped around a heart, the international symbol for healers—and in this case, a sign of illness. What a fascinating, brilliant system. He shuffled through the rest. Green seemed to indicate he would be out, red indicated staying in, yellow seemed to mean 'leave me alone', and blue and purple he could not puzzle out. Surely they could include a guide or something?

Even as he had the thought, though, he spied a piece of paper on the floor. Setting the cards aside he scooped the paper up, and sure enough, there was the guide he'd wanted. Wind or something must have knocked it off the table.

There was an explanation for the cards, which he'd already correctly figured out, and then it listed each color and what it indicated. His guesses were all correct, and blue proved to mean 'not currently in the palace,' and purple meant 'bring additional food for guest'. The cards were to be placed either by certain times for various meals or left indefinitely where applicable.

As he was currently without clothes and didn't see the point in bothering someone to get his one outfit clean in time for dinner, Amador opened his door and slid the card into the slot just below the peephole.

He should write his family about this charming system; it would make life so much easier for the entire palace.

Yawning, he took his hot toddy, which seemed to be almost entirely whiskey, with a touch of lemon and honey, and went to the doors that led, as he'd hoped, to a balcony. It overlooked a modest sized courtyard that was, predictably, redolent in roses, spilling and piling around enormous trees. There were discreet lights and benches. The whole thing must be absolutely beautiful at night, the perfect spot for a secret rendezvous.

Sadness twinged in his chest, furling into a knot of longing. It would be nice to whisked out to a garden for a secret rendezvous. Or even a non-secret one. That required standing out in some way, though. Being witty and charming. Ridiculously attractive. Brilliantly intelligent.

Instead, he was about as average and dull a prince as it was possible to be. His greatest skills were lame attempts at humor and micromanaging everything. He could also run *very* fast if he so much as thought Ottokar might be in the vicinity.

In everything else, his skills ranged from appalling to strictly average. Honestly it was a mystery to no one why he wasn't married yet. Why he thought he could convince the most elusive bachelor of the season to choose him, of all people, was simply the desperation talking.

Stifling a sigh, he leaned on the balcony railing and tried to count how many different roses were present.

Movement caught his eye, however, immediately distracting him. Oh, a royal gardener. Amador would love to ask the gardeners countless questions about what went into attending what must be a million roses, all so varied in size, shape, and color. Did they use the same soil? Different soils? Where did they obtain fertilizer. Were there roses year round? Did they find or specifically breed winter-hardy roses? How many hours a day were spent on just the roses? Was their specific staff for them, or were all the garden staff trained? What were the costs? Did they sell any of them to recoup some of that? How many varieties were edible? How many went off to perfumers and the like?

Blathering on incessantly, his brother would call it. Acting like a servant instead of a prince, his parents would say. Stop embarrassing us, his sisters would say.

Why was it so strange he wanted to *know* things? Shouldn't they understand all the inner workings of the place they called home? If he did somehow wind up marrying the elusive Prince Nazaire, shouldn't he know all the details of the roses that were so central?

Amador stifled another sigh as he watched the gardener work, mind tumbling with questions he'd probably never get to ask anyone.

He'd just gone back to counting rose types when a new figure appeared… and there was no mistaking the clothes and bearing of a fellow royal. Nazaire. Hard to capture details at a distance, but he was handsome, striking, even better than the sketches and single painting that Amador had been sent. He had the soft brown skin common to the kingdom, and his ink-dark hair was pulled back in a short tail, ruthlessly made straight but with the curls fighting their way back out.

"Léonce!" Nazaire said as he spied the gardener, and added with a laugh, "What in the world are you doing all the way over here?"

Léonce looked up, then scrambled to his feet and stood, wiping sweat from his face, but only succeeding in adding dirt. He tipped into a hasty bow. "Your Highness! Um, to be perfectly honest, I'm avoiding Didier. He has some loud opinions on the new maple trees that I disagree with, and I thought it best to avoid the argument altogether."

"Him again?"

"Don't you dare do a thing, Your Highness," Léonce said with a laugh. "I can handle Didier."

Nazaire pouted, of all things. How charming. "Fine, but one of these days, you're going to have to let me terminate that bastard."

"He does his job well, Your Highness, he's merely not pleasant about it. That's hardly a terminating offense. What are *you* doing all the way out here? I thought you had… um, someone else to meet today."

Sighing with a force that would impress Amador's mother, Nazaire dropped onto the nearest bench and rested his chin in one hand. "Tonight at dinner. I was told he has arrived, but that the weather left the poor bastard a right mess." They both looked up at the sky—rather, the glass dome protecting them from the rain still pounding down relentlessly. Thankfully, neither noticed Amador.

"You don't sound enthused, Your Highness. Is this prince no good either?"

"Everything I've heard says he's perfectly fine. Same as all the rest. I'm simply not interested in marrying. I don't care what the stupid council insists upon."

"I'm sorry none of them have worked out, Your Highness." Léonce rose from where he'd been weeding a patch of pink roses and sat slowly, carefully on the bench as well, so close to the edge he'd tumble right off if he wasn't careful.

Amador narrowed his eyes. Léonce didn't sound sorry, not even a little bit. If Amador didn't know better, he'd say Léonce sounded *relieved*. Well, well, well. How delightfully intriguing. Was the charming little gardener smitten with the prince?

Given how familiar the two seemed to be…

"Could be worse," Nazaire said with another sigh. "Sohan could be forcing the matter, but all he's done is ask me to not reject this one immediately."

"Seems crueler to play along for a time."

"That's what I said, but Sohan and his politics," Nazaire replied. "The least I can do is accede to his request. But I shouldn't be out here whining and bothering—"

"Léonce!"

The two men jerked apart like they'd been caught in some smoldering tête-a-tête instead of just sitting at a normal distance having a normal conversation. This just grew more and more delightfully intriguing.

A guard came into view, dressed in armor that was expensive and well-maintained, even at a distance, over it a surcoat of emerald green trimmed in blue and orange. She had skin so pale that snow would look colorful by comparison, and hair nearly the same orange as the trim of her surcoat. "Here you are, you scapegrace! Oh, Your Highness, I beg your pardon." The woman tipped into an elegant bow, one hand resting on the hilt of her sword. "I did not see you there."

"It's fine, Vladlena," Nazaire said. "Why are you hunting down my favorite gardener?"

"Master Didier is wanting to speak with him, Your Highness," Vladlena replied. "Something about the location of the new hydrangea?"

"If he even *thinks* about touching my hydrangea, I will bury him beneath his maples!" Léonce said, and bolted from the garden, leaving Nazaire staring after him, Vladlena laughing loudly, and Amador struggling desperately to smother his own laughter.

As she finally calmed her laughter, Vladlena said, "If you will pardon me, Your Highness, I should probably go after him and avert capital murder."

"Please do."

Vladlena took off, and Nazaire sighed again. He turned away to head back the way he'd come, but stopped and bent, scooping up what looked to be a glove. He stroked his thumb across it, then clenched the glove tightly in his hand before tucking it away in his jacket and striding off.

Well, then. That certainly explained why Nazaire rejected every single suitor that showed up. He was in love with the charming gardener. If Amador wasn't mistaken, the gardener was equally besotted with Nazaire. Neither seemed aware of the other's affections, though. Hmm…

An interesting bit of information to file away, to be sure.

Out of hot toddy and people to shamelessly eavesdrop on, Amador returned to his room, where he was delighted to see that his staff had arrived, sodden and cranky, but with all his belongs more or less intact. "Go get warm and dry, take your time, please," Amador said. "I can handle the unpacking, at least of what I need immediately." When they tried to protest, he said, "I hardly need you dripping water and mud over everything, run along you three."

That defeated them, and the three—Soledad, his secretary; Bibiana, his chamber servant; and Edu, his runner slash general helper—slipped off to obey, leaving him alone with his piles and piles of luggage. Amador had always favored traveling in comfort over traveling light.

Throwing open the various chests, six of them in total, with smaller trunks and bags off to one side, he scrounged up sufficient clothes for the night and morning, along with his small jewelry case and a bag of necessaries. The rest he left, as Bibiana would murder him if he dared to try to put everything away, and he preferred to stay on her good side.

Dressed respectably again, and having already opted out of attending the dinner that would be starting in an hour or so, Amador opted to go exploring.

Where the palace he'd grown up in was an ostentatious nightmare, everything gleaming gold, glittering crystals, and shiny surfaces that showed every hint of smudge, Harridor Palace was warm and friendly, made of gray-brown stone with color everywhere: flowers and other greenery; tapestries and rug; colored and enameled glass; furniture that looked as though someone had remembered comfort mattered…

It felt like the kind of place that could be home, where his own home always felt the world's most uncomfortable hotel.

Sadly, to judge by that little scene in the garden, nobody here would be inviting him to stay. Well, what had he really expected? Success? Desperately hoped for, maybe, but not expected. He simply wasn't the kind of person who was swept up into the arms of his true love mere minutes upon arrival. He didn't get swept up at all. Or even noticed. He was the one in the background making certain there was enough food and wine, that the musicians were all right, that the staff wasn't being overworked, and that nobody had gotten so drunk they fell into the fountain.

He was, in short, the boring one. People expected him to provide the gardens for secret rendezvous, but nobody ever wanted to rendezvous him.

No, the only person who wanted to marry him was a bastard so selfish and cruel that the last time they'd met, he'd thrown a glass bottle so hard the shrapnel had sliced

Amador's arm open. He hadn't even apologized, just blamed Amador for the whole mess.

Amador couldn't wait to be forced into that marriage. Maybe he'd just run away. Linger here as long as he could, be safe and warm for a bit, and then just hie off in a random direction. Maybe he'd find a handsome merchant who wouldn't mind a boring ex-prince who thought making lists was fun.

A worry for later. For now, he was going to enjoy this beautiful palace, and maybe find someone who wouldn't mind Amador asking a thousand questions. Maybe he could find Léonce and learn more about the intriguing tale of the maples, hydrangeas, and the dastardly Didier. Or perhaps he'd chance upon the guard in her beautiful armor, see how she fit—

Laughter, familiar and dreaded, hit him like a fist in the gut. Amador froze as he reached a spot where the hallway divided, one path right, one left. He had to be imagining…

No, there it came again. The familiar low, mean laugh of a gloating Ottokar.

Stomach roiling, Amador looked toward the sound. There he was, the stupid, evil bastard himself. In all his icy beauty, like a frozen lake just waiting to crack beneath the feet of the unwary. He was supposed to be far,

far away, damn it.

Amador turned to go somewhere, anywhere, before he was spotted. By the way Ottokar's laughter abruptly cut off, though, he was too late.

"Amador! Fancy meeting you here."

Amador shot him a look of absolute loathing, then blindly fled, running down the hallway further away from Ottokar, only belatedly realizing that going back the way he'd come would have been smarter. Too late now.

He came to another divide and went left again, turning his head to see if he'd been caught up to yet—and registering an alarmed voice only right as he slammed into someone. Arms wrapped around him, large and warm, comforting in a way he'd never really felt.

Fear and panic fled momentarily as Amador reflexively looked up into a face filled with surprise and concern. The man was handsome, distractingly so, with warm, pale brown skin and eyes the soft green of moss, a faint spray of freckles across his nose and cheeks. He had a close cropped beard and mustache, barely there at all, and lips Amador dare not dwell on, cheekbones that ached to be stroked before some lucky bastard leaned in to steal a kiss.

Then Ottokar's voice came from a distance that was still far too close. "Sorry,"

Amador sputtered, and pushed out of the arms that felt far too safe and steady. "My apologies. I didn't mean— Excuse me, please, I must go." He bolted down the hall, barely hearing as the mystery man first cried for him to wait, then asked, "Who in the world was that?"

Amador kept going, desperate to get away from *him*, the boy who'd beat him up and the student who'd locked him out of his room while completely naked and the man who'd sliced his arm open and there'd been so much fucking blood.

He ran until he was safely behind a massive tree in a garden and didn't breathe properly until several minutes passed without the sound of Ottokar's horrid voice.

When it seemed like he had finally escaped torment, he sank to the ground and folded his arms across his knees and focused solely on his breathing. In one two three. Out one two three. He'd run away and be a prostitute before he'd marry Ottokar. It would certainly be a safer life, and wasn't that telling.

As his heartbeat finally slowed, and the soothing silence stretched on, Amador stretched his legs out, leaned his head against the tree, and folded his hands in his lap. Ottokar's stupid face faded to the background of his mind, and the beautiful stranger he'd crashed into surged to the front.

Who had the man been? Something about him had been vaguely familiar, but try as Amador might, he could not figure out why. Stupidly, he could still feel the man's arms around him, so very warm and steadying. So very *safe*. Like as long as the handsome stranger was right there, Ottokar couldn't come anywhere near him. If only life were that simple. That kind. The King of Portan himself would not be able to keep Ottokar from tormenting Amador.

"Beg pardon, but are you all right?" a voice asked.

Amador jerked to his feet and spun around, heart seizing before he registered the voice was not remotely anything like Ottakar's, far too soft and gentle. It was also familiar. Staring a moment, Amador finally realized why. "You're the gardener."

Léonce blinked. "Yes, I am a gardener. How did you know, erm… my lord?"

"Prince, actually," Amador said with a laugh. "I saw you briefly when I was exploring my chambers and stepped out onto the balcony. You were weeding a bed of roses. Fascinating all the inner gardens have glass over them, so they fare well no matter what the weather. Does that hold true in cold weather?"

"Um—yes, it does, though they take a good deal more work, then. Uh, Your

Highness. Are you all right?"

"I'm fine, thank you. My apologies for barging into your garden."

"Not at all. Gardens are for people, whether to enjoy or to hide in." Léonce smiled fleetingly. "You'd be surprised how many people throughout the day, from the night collectors to even His Majesty, retreat to the gardens every day. It's why I'm quite proud to be a gardener."

"You should be," Amador said. "They're beautiful. I've heard about the roses of Harridor, but never about all the other plants and trees and flowers here." He smiled faintly and chanced, "I saw some lovely hydrangea earlier."

Léonce's face lit up. "I'm delighted you enjoyed them, Your Highness. They're imported from Karlow, just arrived last week, and I thought they'd do the Maiden Fountain justice."

"You thought correctly." At least Amador had a real goal for tomorrow now. "I am sorry all the same to interrupt whatever you are working on here." He finally gave a good look to the garden he'd fled to, which featured a weeping willow in pride of place, draped over a pond filled with pink and white fish. "Another beautiful space. You have an instinct for the work."

Flushing, Léonce replied, "Thank you,

Your Highness. Would you like me to have tea or wine or something brought?"

"You know, wine would be marvelous. Thank you." Amador hesitated, then decided his day couldn't possibly get worse and asked, "Are you terribly busy? I'd love to hear more details about the famous roses and everything else you work on. Most people don't see the point of telling a prince the details of the pretty things we look at all day, but it must be quite the task to maintain such beautiful gardens."

Léonce smiled as bright as the sun, and it wasn't hard at all to see why Nazaire was in love with him. "It would be my honor, Your Highness, just let me call for your wine."

"Thank you, I deeply appreciate it. Make certain there is enough for two. I would never be so rude to drink alone in front of others."

"Yes, Your Highness," Léonce said with a laugh, and went off to see to the wine.

Introductions

The morning arrived full of sunshine and promise. Amador dressed in his favorite bottle green jacket with matching black and green boots. A little flashy, but he needed all the help he could get in that regard. Unlike his siblings, who had the black-brown skin that was so highly regarded back home, his was more of a dull medium with even duller undertones. He wasn't ugly, but nobody described him as beautiful or striking or even interesting either. Passable was usually the kindest he got. His mother often wondered, loudly but seldom to his face, how she'd wound up with four beautiful children and one so homely.

With an endorsement like that, was it really so shocking nobody wanted to marry him?

Moot point, now, since his options were

firmly down to Ottokar or running away, which meant his options were run away now or run away later. *Now* would be the smart thing, but he was far too invested in the tale of the prince and the gardener to abandon it.

So he would go see the hydrangea he'd told Léonce he loved, then more of the gardens Léonce had told him about, and once the morning court began, he would finally present himself properly, meet the other player in this secret little romance he was spying on. Perhaps contrive a plot to give their mutual pining a happy end.

There was certainly something to be said for strolling a beautiful palace redolent with the scent of roses. He liked even better the way people seemed so relaxed, instead of moving quietly and stiffly through the halls, afraid of doing anything that might displease the royal family or any of their cronies.

Amador *really* did not miss home. He would do anything, short of marrying Ottokar, to never see home again.

Hopefully there was a merchant out there who would be utterly enchanted by his ability to balance a ledger and his extensive knowledge of tax laws.

His thoughts slid away as he turned down a hallway and spied the archway that Léonce had talked about avidly: trees that had been carefully twined and twisted together as they grew, shaped to form a natural archway before growing up and out again, making an entrance even grander than the one fronting the palace.

Stepping through it, he looked over what Léonce had called the Dancing Garden, named for the fountains that served as centerpieces: a fountain of young men dancing, a fountain depicting young women dancing, and a third that was children of all shapes and sizes. With the triangle of fountains as a focal point, the garden spilled out to the walls that encircled it, and even up them in beautiful jewel-toned ivies and flowers.

As Amador had assured Léonce was the case sight unseen, the hydrangea around the fountain of dancing women were indeed lovely, bursts of soft pastels that added a whimsical flair to everything. The hotly contested maples were nowhere to be seen, so Léonce must have won his fight. Around the remaining fountains was only earth, so either more hydrangea were going in soon, or the matter had yet to be settled.

He'd never been involved in garden drama before; what charming fun this was proving to be. Amador laughed softly as he thought about how charming the poor gardeners did *not* find the drama.

Making a note to find Léonce later in

the day and tell him again just how beautiful the hydrangea were, he continued on, leaving the Dancing Garden behind and going left through a brick archway into what Léonce had called the Fish Garden.

As promised, it did indeed contain a great many fish, scattered across multiple ponds. He could also hear frogs ribbiting away, and insects buzzing and humming. The ponds also had floating plants that he'd never seen before, not outside books and paintings, anyway. He lingered to admire the fish in each pond, then moved on again, eager to get to what Léonce had called the Rainbow Garden.

Amador laughed in delight as he stepped through yet another archway and came upon it. The Rainbow Garden very much lived up to its name, a splendid display of roses in every imaginable color, arranged in loose circular fashion in the very order of a rainbow. He hoped whoever had designed this had been properly rewarded for it. Léonce, maybe? But he'd said he was a lower ranking gardener, not a master or head gardener, who did the designing. Still, it really had seemed…

Well, who knew. One more question for which to seek an answer.

He continued on his way through the Rainbow Garden, admiring every single shade of rose, especially the blue and purple, which he'd never seen before. He hadn't thought roses came in those colors, but here they were, vivid and stunning.

There was also another pond, this one filled with tiny fish that looked like chips of rainbow themselves. Must be a lot of additional work to care for the fish in addition to the flowers. Where did they get the fish? Caught in the wild? Bred specially? Shipped in from afar somehow? What went into caring for them? Did different fish require different kinds of water, and plants in and around their pond? What did they—

Voices, one familiar, snapped Amador from his musings. Prince Nazaire, speaking with… They were tucked amidst some trees and shrubs, but he could just barely see them seated on a bench. A noblewoman, he thought, that was the other person.

"—asleep again!

The noblewoman laughed. "Why do you ever think you can stay awake? You're not a night owl, Nazaire!"

"You could help me, you know," Nazaire replied sourly. "Instead of just laughing at me all the time."

Snapping a fan open, the woman fluttered it in front of her face. "Secret admirers are *secret*, darling. If they wanted you to know their identity, they'd approach you directly, not sneak into your room to leave you roses and love notes."

"What's the point of saying anything at all if they're never going to give me a chance to return their affections?"

The woman snorted. "Ah, yes, because you've made such a show of being willing to return affections, what with casting out one suitor after another. So approachable."

"Oh, shut up and go away if you're just going to lambast me. I can't help I don't want any of these would-be suitors. Isn't it better to be direct about it than give them false hope?"

"That's not the point, dear," the woman said with a sigh. "The point is you've made yourself unapproachable."

Nazaire groaned and buried his head in his hands.

"I think I hear the familiar rattle of your brother's guards," the woman said.

"Oh, good, just what I needed to complete my morning: yet another lecture about being nice to this latest suitor."

Amador withdrew. He really needed to stop making a habit of accidentally eavesdropping on people. It was rude and going to get him in trouble. On the other hand, at least he knew what he was truly facing and wouldn't waste time on a hopeless courtship. No, he'd focus on helping—

Hands shoved him from behind, hard enough to bruise, jolting through his back and even down his arms, sending him slamming into the pond with a resounding smack.

Amador cried out, and then promptly choked on water as he flailed to sort out up from down, get his bearings, get the fish out of his jacket, which was now *ruined*.

Then strong hands gripped him, hauled him to his feet, and Amador once more found himself staring into moss-green eyes set in an unfairly handsome face. Wonderful. The only thing better than making a fool of himself was *repeatedly* making a fool of himself. "I'm so sorry," he rasped out, coughing out the last of the water. "I don't—"

"Shh, don't talk, give yourself a moment to get your breath back," the man said, his voice deep and warm, as beautiful as the rest of him.

Wiping water from his face, shoving his ruined hair from his eyes, Amador finally got a proper look at this man who'd seen him being hopelessly stupid twice now.

A crown. The man was wearing a crown. How had he missed that before?

Amador's heart dropped into his stomach. He was making a perfect fool of himself in front of *King Sohan*.

Why couldn't the stupid bastard who'd pushed him have been kind enough to finish the job?

'The stupid bastard.' Like he didn't know. *Why* was a mystery, but only one person in the palace would want to push Amador into a pond.

Amador couldn't decide if he wanted to burst into tears or throw himself back into the pond.

"I'm so sorry," he finally said. They were up to their thighs in the water. His clothes were ruined, and worse, His Majesty's clothes were ruined. "Your Majesty, I swear I don't mean to keep troubling you. Are you all right?"

"Am *I* all right?" Sohan laughed, and shifted to put Amador at his side, sliding an arm loosely around his waist, and guided him to the edge of the pond. "You're the one who took a spill, Your Highness. Are *you* all right?"

"Nothing wounded but pride and dignity." Amador made to climb out himself, but two soldiers, likely bodyguards, grabbed hold and hauled him out like he weighed nothing. "Thank you, Your Majesty. I truly am sorry to have bothered you with my clumsiness."

Sohan frowned. "Clumsiness? That's not what it seemed like to me, especially combined with yesterday."

He hadn't even been at Harridor Palace a full day, and already Ottokar was ruining everything. "I assure you that I'm my own worst enemy, Your Majesty. You must tell me how I can make amends for being so rude and troublesome."

Sohan's frown deepened, but he only said, "What I want is to hear the truth of the matter, but we'll discuss that later. I'll see you at breakfast, Your Highness." He motioned to his bodyguards, which numbered six in total, and two of them parted from the others as the rest escorted Sohan away, trailed by a wide-eyed Nazaire and his friend, who regarded Amador far more pensively than he liked.

Swallowing the thorny lump in his throat, he sloughed more water from his clothes as best he could, removed his sodden boots so he wouldn't ruin the floors again, and headed off. The bodyguards followed him, but Amador didn't have the stomach to ask them why or tell them not to bother. All he wanted was to find the nearest hole in the ground and crawl into it.

Instead, he returned to his rooms, waved off the alarm of his staff, and got cleaned up and freshly dressed. So much for his favorite jacket. The delicate velvet was not made to endure such a rough and thorough soaking, so off to the scrap heap it would have to go.

A stupid thing to be so upset over, but he had truly loved that jacket.

And as long as he focused on the jacket, he wouldn't think about looking like the stupidest, most helpless person in the world in front of King Sohan. Thank the gods he didn't actually need to convince Nazaire to marry him, because if that had still been the plan, it would be utterly ruined.

Staring at himself in the mirror, Amador fussed with his clothes, jewels, and hair, as though he might magically come upon some tweak that would make him beautiful and alluring, so appealing that King Sohan would forget all about princes crashing into him and practically drowning in front of him.

Ugh. What did he even care what King Sohan thought? What any of them thought? He was lingering because he was a hopeless romantic who wanted to see if he could get the gardener and his prince together. That hardly required impressing anyone, least of all a king.

Even if he was a stupidly handsome king with lovely eyes and strong, warm arms, who was kind enough to fish a stupid prince from a pond himself—

Ugh. Whatever. Amador jerked away from the mirror, ignored the concerned stares of his staff, and stepped into dove gray buckled shoes that matched his breeches and dusty lavender jacket. Not nearly as handsome as the bottle green one, but it would suffice for making him presentable.

If only he could have managed to look impressive.

Amador shoved the useless, treacherous thought aside. He didn't need to look impressive, and he didn't want to look impressive. Presentable was more than good enough.

"I've no idea when I'll be back, so feel free to spend your days however you like," Amador said, mustering a smile for his staff, the only three people in the world who'd chosen *him* instead of his family. "Thank you, for everything. I always appreciate everything you three do. I wouldn't be here without you."

"We hope your day improves, Your Highness," said Edu, and the other two bobbed their heads in agreement.

"Thank you." Amador departed—and drew up short in the hallway as he saw the two bodyguards remained right where he'd left them. "Oh, I'm sorry. I didn't realize you'd be waiting for me, or I'd have been quicker about getting cleaned up and dressed again."

The guards seemed faintly amused, but the taller of the two only said, "His Majesty bid us escort you until told otherwise. We serve at your pleasure, Your Highness; there's no need to hurry on our behalf. Shall we on to the dining hall?"

"Yes, please, thank you."

Why in the world would His Majesty assign his own bodyguards to follow Amador around? Had he proven to be so alarmingly incompetent he needed to be protected from himself?

The urge to ask them to find Ottokar and beat him out of existence was strong, but Amador couldn't truly bring himself to request outright murder, even if Ottokar's death would only bring more peace to the world.

Instead he walked in silence, mentally rehearsing all the things he would like to say, charmingly and effortlessly, to His Majesty while knowing full well he'd just fumble all of it and sound like an utter cake.

"I'm a royal prince, I can act like it," Amador muttered to himself.

He swore one of the guards snorted, but before he could figure it out for certain, they were sweeping through the enormous open double doors of the dining hall. Being a prince of no consequence, Amador could have picked any available seat, but the bodyguards swept him onward through the room, right up to the royal table, where he was all but shoved into a chair directly across from King Sohan and Prince Nazaire.

"Um, good morning, Your Majesty, Your Highness. I apologize again for my shameful clumsiness from earlier. You did not have to put guards on me."

Looking faintly amused, probably because he knew full well he didn't have to do anything he didn't want, Sohan replied, "After yesterday's fright and today's assault, I want to ensure such things don't happen a third time. I'll not have my guests so mistreated, least of all by other guests."

Wonderful, he'd somehow sussed out at least some of the truth of the matter, that Amador was utterly useless and pathetic whenever Ottokar was even remotely nearby. "It's my own carelessness to blame, nothing more," Amador said anyway.

Sohan's mouth tightened, but he only said, "I hope you are unhurt from your fall?"

"I'm hale and hearty, Your Majesty. I'm sorry for the trouble I've caused you, truly."

Next to Sohan, Nazaire snorted a laugh. "Trouble. Hardly, Your Highness. If you want to see what trouble really looks like, you should attend the council meeting this afternoon. As my guest, even." He grinned. "I would be honored."

"The honor would be mine," Amador said, not certain what else to say, feeling very much like he was missing something. "Still, it cannot be every day His Majesty ruins his own clothes and wastes his valuable time fishing clumsy princes from fishponds."

"You'd be surprised," Sohan said dryly. "Enough of that, though. You come from Tesh Kingdom, Your Highness, do you not?"

"Yes, Your Majesty. I am right in the middle of five children, the most...

wandering, I suppose, of the lot."

"I met your eldest brother, the crown prince, some years ago. He was intense," Sohan replied.

A laugh escaped before Amador could restrain it, sharp and ugly. Well, may as well accept it. "That's the kindest synonym for 'domineering ass' that I've ever heard, Your Majesty."

Sohan stared at him a moment, then laughed himself. "You're refreshing, Your Highness."

Well, that was better than most 'compliments' he received. "You'll change your mind once I start rambling about tax law, don't worry."

That made Sohan frown ever so briefly, but before he could comment, Nazaire said, "Funny you should mention tax law, Your Highness—"

"Please, you may use my name, I see little sense in formality after falling face first into a pond and having the king himself fish me out." Amador drew a deep breath and let it out slowly, silently, wishing harder than ever for that hole to crawl into.

Silence hung over the table for a moment, and then it was Sohan who said, "Amador, correct? Amador Sanz."

"Yes," Amador said, feeling gutted and bereft for no good reason at all. He wanted, viscerally, desperately, to hear Sohan say his name softly, in the intimacy of a bedroom or a garden rendezvous. To feel those arms around him because Sohan had chosen to hold him close, not because Amador had barreled into him in a moment of panicked inattention.

People like Sohan, beautiful and charismatic, didn't waste their time on people Amador, plain and boring, though. Amador would have more luck seducing the prince already in love with the gardener.

Sohan smiled. "It is a pleasure to have you here, quite different from the usual sort who come to woo my brother."

Amador returned the smile. "The pleasure is all mine, to simply be in such pleasant company, and to have so many beautiful gardens to peruse. I chanced upon one of your gardeners last night, name of Léonce, and he was delighted to tell me all about them." There was no missing the happiness and longing that filled Nazaire's brown eyes then, but Amador didn't press. Patience was the key to this plot. Patience and slow, steady steps. "I apologize, though, you were saying something about taxes?"

"My favorite breakfast topic," Sohan drawled.

Nazaire laughed. "That's good, because it's all the council talks about anymore. They're in a tizzy about some new law or addendum or what have you."

"The Filandra Amendment," Amador said, excited and hating himself for it. "It's an anti-avoidance amendment to international tax law; scores of businesses and countries can no longer use some rather useful loopholes to dodge paying taxes. There's also a vote happening soon that will determine if the dodged taxes will have to be paid, or if the slate will simply be wiped clean. A handful of countries, including Partin of course, are unaffected by it, but individual businesses within basically *all* countries will be heavily impacted. There's great fear many will be forced into bankruptcy or otherwise compelled to close. I'd be surprised if Your Majesty's council *wasn't* alarmed; the economic ramifications are going to be…"

They stared at him, silent, and new cracks formed in Amador's heart. Why couldn't he ever keep his stupid mouth shut? He just… wanted to be useful…but he'd chosen all the most boring ways to do that. Nobody wanted a prince who rambled about tax law. They had tax clerks for that.

He dropped his gaze to his plate, no longer hungry. "Apologies, it really is a terrible topic for breakfast." For any meal, or not meal.

Sohan replied, "Actually—"
"Your Majesty."

Amador looked up just in time to see the barest hint of annoyance pass over Sohan's face before he replied to the man who'd interrupted them, "Yes, Lord Lipovsky? What is it?"

It was hard not to stare, given the man's shockingly familiar snow-pale skin and fiery orange hair. Amador focused on his tea before he got caught staring.

Lipovsky bowed slightly in apology and said, "I was wondering if you could spare a moment of your time, Your Majesty. There's an urgent matter I need to speak to you about."

"I'll speak with you at the end of the hour, in my office," Sohan replied. When Lipovsky had gone, he pushed away from the table. "Which means I must attend to a different matter now. I beg your pardon, Prince Amador. I'll see you at…lunch? No, more likely dinner. Have a good day." He winked. "Stay away from ponds." He strode off before Amador could reply, his bodyguards folding in around him.

"That was impressive, you know," Nazaire said.

Amador's gaze snapped to him. "What was? Falling into a pond? Anyone can do it. I'll be happy to teach you."

Nazaire laughed, happy and bright, not a trace of artifice in it. Eyes sparkling, he finally said, "No, not that, tempting though your offer is, Your Highness—pardon, Amador. I was speaking of all that tax stuff you rattled off. I fell asleep whenever the tutors started in on it. I don't think Sohan was any better. How did you manage to stay awake through it all?"

"I like knowing how things work," Amador said, staring at his plate again.

"Some people enjoy the painting," Nazaire said, and something about his tone of voice drew Amador's gaze up again, "and some enjoy the painting, as it were." He winked, very much like his brother, and yet not the same at all.

Amador smiled, something very much like cautious hope blooming in his chest. "Well said, Your Highness."

"A touch awkward, but I'm glad the point carried," Nazaire said, beaming. "Dare I hope you're not going to force me to reject you?"

"No worries there, Your Highness," Amador said, forcing a smile he only sort of felt. "It's the travel that interests me, not the courting. I knew before I arrived that my chances were essentially zero. I assume your interest lies elsewhere, or you have no interest whatsoever—and it's not for me to ask, and I'm not."

Nazaire's smile turned into a strangely mischievous grin. "That's good. I don't think certain parties would take it well if I was the competition. I'm always happy to make a friend, though."

"Good friends are hard to find." What in the world did the rest of what he'd said mean? "Actually, if you don't mind, I had a rather strange question regarding that man who wanted to speak with His Majesty."

"Lipovsky?" Nazaire's nose wrinkled. "What in the world do you want to know about him?"

"Honestly, it's probably a stupid question, and my ignorance as a foreigner will show itself, but he looked almost exactly like a guard I passed by earlier. The same pale skin and striking red hair, and the unusual names…"

Nazaire's expression cleared. "Oh, crossed paths with Vladlena, did you? There are rumors to her parentage, but nothing acknowledged. A pity, because she would do the family name well, and he lacks for heirs, but…" He shrugged one shoulder, a wealth of meaning in the gesture, speaking of nobles, bloodlines, and snobbery.

So she was a bastard child. Interesting. He doubted that was at all useful to his cause, but it was information to file away all the same.

A prince in love with a gardener. A gardener in love with a prince. A gardener good friends with the bastard child of a noble powerful enough he could interrupt the king's breakfast, but not so powerful he'd do it through servants.

Amador crossed his silverware over his empty plate and finished his tea. "I'm certain you've a busy day ahead of you, Your Highness—"

"Nazaire, please," Nazaire said with a smile. "Not as busy as that. Would you like a tour of the palace? I promise we'll stay away from ponds."

"I'm never going to hear the end of that," Amador said with a sigh, though a smile twitched at his mouth. It was nice to be teased about such things, instead of reprimanded, even if he could still feel the bruising force of Ottokar's shove.

Nazaire snickered as he rose. "Neither is Sohan. His bodyguards were ready to kill him. Shall we tour, then?"

"That sounds marvelous," Amador said, standing and accepting the arm that Nazaire offered.

He'd failed before he'd begun at his last chance for a spouse that wasn't Ottokar, but it was nice to have a friend for as long as he was here. Who knew, maybe if his scheming succeeded, they'd find him so amazingly clever and wonderful they'd insist he stay to help them with other matters.

The idea was absurd, but most would say so was the thought of a prince marrying a gardener.

Maybe it was, but Amador enjoyed writing lists and reading about tax law. He knew all about absurd.

More Mischief

"La, darling, there you are," said a playful, familiar voice, right before a woman looped her arm through Nazaire's, casual as she pleased. "I was starting to think you were abandoning me to suffer this meeting alone."

The woman from the garden. Amador hadn't gotten a good look at her, but he'd know that voice.

She was as beautiful as the company she kept, with springy brown curls she'd twined into a fancy twist that looked as though it would come apart at any moment. Her medium brown skin had rich red undertones, and the freckles across her nose and cheeks gave an innocent look to her features, even as her eyes danced with curiosity and mischief. She wore a green gown with gold trim, beautifully tailored to her flat chest and narrow hips, the skirt not quite touching the floor, pulled slightly up in tufts that revealed a purple underskirt. She fluttered a matching fan, then gestured to Amador. "Who's your handsome new friend?"

"Prince Amador Sanz of Tesh, I make you known to Lady Marcellette Babineaux, eldest daughter and heir of Lord Babineaux, Duke of Montagne LeRoux, and my oldest and dearest friend. She is also a mistress of mischief, of the highest order, so do be wary."

"I was never troubled by mischief, so long as it brings no harm," Amador said, bowing over the hand she offered.

Marcellette scoffed. "Mischief that brings harm is just bullying."

"Well said, my lady," Amador replied with a smile. "So what is so exciting about today's council meeting that Nazaire would invite me as his guest?"

"They're in a tizzy over that tax amendment, and there's also a matter pertaining to Baron Pelletier that is being discussed today, though I doubt it'll resolve before they waste at least half a dozen of these meetings. Amusing, given how angry everyone was forty years ago when the title was given to the Lipovsky family."

"The man from this morning?" Amador asked.

"Oh, met him already, have you?"

Before Nazaire or Amador could reply,

bells rang, sharp and jarring, bringing the room to order.

It was an ornate, almost ostentatious room, the walls covered in dark blue velvet with thick gold stripes spaced widely apart, landscapes in fancy frames in the spaces between. The double doors that led into the room were heavy, made of solid wood carved with the royal crest of a unicorn surrounded by a wreath of, predictably, roses. The carpet was a darker shade of blue, and it matched the padding of the twenty-three chairs around the table, ten on each long side, two at one end, and a single chair, more ornate than the others, at the other end.

Amador sat with many others up in the gallery, observers, not participants. Much like back home, the council discussions were a matter of public record, and so the public was allowed to attend. The reality was that the gallery was filled almost entirely with nobles and others of a certain amount of wealth, and they gathered there to whisper and plot and make quiet deals.

"You're not expected to be at the table?" Amador asked in low tones that wouldn't carry in a room where voices were meant to do precisely that.

Nazaire scoffed. "No. I attend as often as I can to keep properly apprised, but Sohan doesn't require I be down there, as I'm not his heir. Well, the law will dictate I am if he doesn't produce one within the next five years, but..." He shrugged. "That's not a problem yet."

What an interesting and oddly useful law. "Does that law apply only to the royal family?"

"No, it applies to all the noble houses, though the rules are a touch intricate," Marcellette replied, snapping her fan closed and leaning forward slightly, adding in a murmur, "Here we go..."

Down below, various nobles had filed in and were taking their seats, as servants brought them various drinks before moving to take their places against the wall.

Portan was a small kingdom, divided into ten provinces, and those provinces further broken down as needed. Each province had two representatives on the royal council. The two seats at the side nearest the door were occupied by the Minister of the Treasury and the Minister of State.

The remaining, and grandest, seat was positioned farthest from the door and with the clearest view of the room, his back to the only wall that had no gallery. Everyone rose as Sohan entered, flanked by his bodyguards as ever, and took his seat.

Once everyone was seated again, the bells rang a second time. A handsome woman stepped up to stand to the right and slightly behind Sohan, sliding reading glasses on her nose before she read from the papers on the board in her hands. In a brisk voice, she read off a summary of the last meeting's minutes, followed by the agenda for that day, which mostly sounded like minor matters. There was definitely stirring as the amendment matter was read off, and whispers as she ended with 'the succession of the Barony Pelletier'.

"Of course, they're putting them last," Marcellette muttered, folding her arms across her chest. "Jerks."

Nazaire snorted a laugh into his hand. "Behave."

"I'm far too beautiful to behave, darling."

That just made Nazaire struggle more than ever to contain his laugh. Marcellette grinned before turning her attention back to the meeting.

They moved swiftly through the minor orders of business, mostly allotment of funds, adjustments to local laws, and a change in how yearly taxes were to be collected to make things easier for provincial areas.

Everyone seemed to stir and buzz as that matter was finally closed, and the clerk called the next matter. She'd barely finished announcing it when the table launched into an argument they had clearly all been champing at the bit to begin.

Marcellette whistled. "Minister Royer is going to get fined for using that kind of language."

"Oh, no, stop, not his pocket change," Nazaire replied.

Down below, Sohan gave the barest glance up at the three of them before he put his attention back on the meeting. The ministers were practically shouting now, but Sohan only watched, quiet and pensive.

"Caught," Nazaire said with a sigh. "I swear he has ears like a cat."

"I think he's just well-attuned to his siblings causing even the slightest hint of trouble," Marcellette replied. "In his defense, you once bellowed that Minister St. Martin was…oh, how did you put it… an officious twat with brains more full of holes that Antour cheese."

Nazaire spread his hands. "He was just mad I was right."

Amador bit his cheek to keep from laughing out loud. "That could describe any number of Ministers, at least the ones I've met. Though honestly, many of them better deserve to be described as the thieving rats running off with the cheese."

"What an image," Marcellette said dryly. "Let's quit with the comparisons while we're ahead. Ooohhh…"

Below, Sohan had lifted a hand, causing silence to ripple down the length of the table. "Your bickering is accomplishing nothing. I hear a great deal of blame-placing and a lot of defensive reactions and excuses, but I've yet to hear anyone offer even the barest solution. The amendment will pass. The international council convenes in three days for the final vote, and it's closing an important loophole in international tax law. Pretending otherwise is a waste of time, and I'm not going to sit here and waste more of mine."

"But—" The woman who had started to speak snapped her mouth shut at the look Sohan gave her.

"His Majesty is good at that," Amador said, unable to tear his eyes away. "My parents can silence a room rather effectively, but not the way he does." No, his parents silenced through sheer terror. If Amador was not the boring middle child nobody really cared about, he'd have been subjected to much, much worse. His eldest siblings had been ruthlessly molded, and his younger siblings were little more than chess pieces, already locked into marriages advantageous to the throne and absolutely no one and nothing else.

Really, the only reason his parents had given him time to find a spouse of his own was because they knew it was a waste of time, and at the very least he'd build relationships as he traveled around before returning home to face the inevitable fate of Ottokar.

Running off to seduce a merchant with his bookkeeping skills was looking increasingly appealing.

Not as appealing as a handsome king holding sway over his ministers through skill and respect, who had marvelous warm, strong arms and a deep, soothing voice, but Amador preferred to keep his hopes and expectations realistic.

"He gets it from our mother," Nazaire replied. "She was an excellent queen, and Sohan looked up to her, even as a child. I was too little to remember her, but he was old enough, and works hard to be the kind of king she'd want him to be."

Amador stifled a sigh, not even certain why he wanted to sigh, and only said softly, "I would say he is succeeding."

Nazaire laughed. "Sohan will be delighted to hear you think so. All I've heard since yesterday is—"

"Your Highness, beg pardon for the interruption."

Amador turned away from the meeting and stared at Vladlena, who rose from her bow and continued, "There is a minor disturbance in the offices that requires your attention."

"Of course," Nazaire said. "I'll be back

soon, my friends, or see you later in the day. You can linger, Vladlena, I hardly need an escort to the offices."

Silence fell as Nazaire departed, though given the way Vladlena and Marcellette were staring at each other, there was clearly an intense conversation going on all the same. "You left early," Marcellette said coolly.

"I had duties to attend—I promise, that's not an excuse. Misha came for me."

"Very well," Marcellette replied, and fanned herself. "I presume you'll be present tonight, so we might revisit our conversation?"

"There's nothing to revisit."

Marcellette snapped her fan shut and sharply waved Vladlena off with it. "We'll just see about that. Go be infuriatingly stubborn somewhere else."

"My lady," Vladlena said stiffly, looking briefly hurt before she turned sharply on her heel and strode off.

Curiosity helplessly piqued, Amador said, "That was a curious conversation."

"Frustrating is more like it," Marcellette said with a sigh, opening her fan again. "Vladlena is nothing if not stubborn, no matter how logical an argument you present to her. No matter how much easier and grander life would be if the damned woman would just listen to me!"

Amador smiled. "I see."

Marcellette slid him a look, eyes glittering and pensive over the edge of her fan before she snapped it shut. "I rather think you do."

"Let me guess: she is not nobility, and so will not consider the offer I suspect you've made."

"You do indeed see."

"Seems to be a fair bit of that sort of thing around here."

Marcellette's brows shot up. "Oh? What gossip do *you* know that I do not, my dear new arrival?"

"Oh, I think you know it." Amador's smile widened, unable to resist the thrill of a possible co-conspirator. "Let's say I was wandering the gardens and saw some things."

Snorting in unladylike fashion, Marcellette rolled her eyes. "They're a pair, aren't they? Staring right at each other with puppy eyes and everyone but them notices. You're an astute little bastard, Your Highness."

"Amador, please."

She grinned, all mischief and delight. "If you really want to see something interesting, meet me in the blue garden about a quarter to midnight."

The gong sounded, signaling the end of the debate, drawing their attention back to the meeting. The clerk called out the final issue, which was about the Barony Pelletier.

"Baron Pelletier, you are without an heir, and in ten days you will have exceeded the grace period you were granted," Sohan said. "I sympathize, I do, as I am facing much the same myself, though I have a few years yet. Have you any heirs in mind?"

"Not at this time, though I am still pursuing a couple of possibilities. If I could have—"

"No," Sohan said. "We've granted you leniency twice already, more than is typically granted anyone. In ten days, when this council reconvenes, you will present an heir or accept those chosen for you. Per the requirements of the law, the council will appoint an heir and a spare. Councilors, present your candidates and explain your decisions."

"Such an intriguing law, I've never seen its like," Amador said as he sat back, letting the debate wash over him as the various names meant little to him. "What provoked it? I cannot think the nobility were pleased."

Marcellette fanned herself. "Amusingly, it was the nobility that forced it through, several generations ago, to prevent a rather cretinous woman the king had designated his heir from taking the throne. It was a good decision, because she was very much the backstabbing traitor everyone suspected, but the caveat to ramming the law through was that it applied to the noble houses in addition to the royal house. For the most part it works well, but I am concerned with this one. Many of us are."

"Oh?"

"Pelletier lands provide a great deal of fishing and other resources found in the lakes and rivers that span them. They also have access to a mountain pass that is crucial to a popular trade route, and those very same mountains provide still more important crops that only grow in that climate. All in all, it's a lucrative estate, more than you'd expected of a barony, so to say it's coveted..." Marcellette pursed her lips. "Everyone down there is hoping to get hold of it for themselves via their puppet of choice."

Amador frowned. "Why not appoint his own kin? Is there some reason he won't consider the woman who is clearly his own flesh and blood?"

Marcellette looked briefly sad before saying, "Her mother was a prostitute. High-end, well-respected in the city where she worked, but a prostitute all the same. That snotty bastard Lipovsky won't tolerate it, though he's no happier with the situation he's in. Rumors are that he's been trying to cut deals of his own, but what can he offer that they can get by bypassing him entirely? Ah, looks like we're finished for the day. Would you like to join me for refreshments?"

"That sounds delightful." Amador rose and cast his eyes down to the table—and froze, face going hot as he saw that Sohan was staring at them. "Did we do something wrong?"

"Wrong?" Marcellette stared blankly, then followed his gaze and laughed. "I don't think that's the look of a man who sees something *wrong*."

Amador tore his gaze from Sohan. "What?"

Marcellette just smirked and laughed some more, then took his arm. "Come along, it's long past time for something fruity and alcoholic."

"I do rather like the sound of that." Out in the hallway, Marcellette chatted with and introduced Amador to many of the milling councilors and other figures, making their way slowly down the hall. Near the end, they ran into Lord Lipovsky, who bowed upon seeing them. "Your Highness, my lady, I hope the day finds you well."

Acknowledging the bow with a nod, Marcellette replied, "Very well, indeed. I'm sorry your day is not the same, but I hope you have some suitable options for an heir, now?"

"Many options, my lady, thank you," Lipovsky said with a smile that didn't quite hide the bite in each word.

Marcellette's smile was even sharper, but she only said pleasantly, "Have you met His Highness?"

"I have not had the honor."

"Prince Amador Sanz of Tesh, I make you known to Lord Ignatiy Lipovsky, the Baron Pelletier. Lord Lipovsky, His Highness Prince Amador Sanz."

"A pleasure to meet you, Your Highness. I've heard much of your homeland, and of you and your extensive travels."

"I'm flattered," Amador replied. "I hope your current troubles find a solution that brings you joy."

"Thank you."

"Good luck with choosing a candidate," Marcellette replied. "If you will excuse us, my lord, we must be off."

"Of course. Good day, Your Highness, my lady."

They walked off, and as they turned onto a hallway empty, save for a couple of bustling servants, Marcellette said, "I want to punch that blowhard in his stupid, stubborn face. All he has to do is adopt Vladlena as his heir, and all his problems would go away! All Vladlena has to do is agree to marry me, and he'd adopt her faster than he could sign the papers. They certainly have their hard heads in common."

Amador laughed. "Well, I have every

faith you shall come out the victor. I know that much about you, despite the briefness of our acquaintance."

She grinned, fierce and determined. "I do like you, Amador. I like you very much. I think you will do nicely here, especially given the eyes you've already captured."

"The eyes…? What are you—" Amador stopped, the words fleeing his head, as Ottokar stepped into their path.

From around and behind them, the bodyguards Sohan had assigned moved forward and closer, forming a protective circle.

Ottokar's brows rose, the cold, haughty look that Amador despised falling over his face. "What is this nonsense? I am permitted to speak with my betrothed, you blustering thugs."

Fury filled Amador, even as he quailed against being anywhere near Ottokar and the painful, spiteful things he would do just for the fun of it. "I am *not* your betrothed."

"Say what you like," Ottokar replied, sounding ominously annoyed. "You can run around the world all you please, but you know where you will end up. It's been decided for years."

Amador's face burned to be so brazenly humiliated in public, in front of his new friend, Sohan's bodyguards. Over and over, all he did was come out looking like a pathetic fool. "I've agreed to nothing, and I've certainly signed no papers. I'll surrender everything I own and live on the streets before I marry you, Ottokar."

"It's inevitable and you know it." Ottokar smiled, cold and mean. "Keep struggling, though, if it pleases you." *We both know I enjoy it.*

"You will leave, or you will be made to leave," one of the bodyguards said. "By order of His Majesty the King. Do not forget you are a guest here, Your Highness, and His Majesty bid you keep in mind that your permission to be here is tenuous at best. Approach Prince Amador again, for any reason, and you will be removed."

"You do not get to talk to me that way, I don't care whose words you're parroting, you mongrel guard dog. This is personal business, and you'll stay out of it."

The guard who'd spoken, a tall, fierce and imposing woman, stepped forward, right into Ottokar's space, looming over him like he was a child. "Last warning, Your Highness."

Ottokar scoffed—and then stepped back and turned away, leaving Amador reeling and almost faint. "We'll speak later, Amador."

"Fuck, and here I am whining about my petty problems," Marcellette replied, fanning herself rapidly. "Are you really betrothed to him? Because if so, I highly recommend you go with the living on the streets plan."

"Not officially, but our families have been discussing the matter since we were children. I think they hoped we would become good friends, then lovers, so on and so forth. Unfortunately, Ottokar only loves being a malicious cretin. I am sorry you had to see all that. He's not normally so direct in front of strangers."

Marcellette's mouth pinched. "No, I imagine not. His sort prefer to do their deeds in private, where nobody will catch them out. I wonder what has tipped the scales. Not that it matters, since His Majesty is clearly not about to tolerate his nonsense. He'll definitely want to hear about this, so hopefully he'll join us for drinks like he usually does after these meetings."

Amador had never been so certain of something in his life as he was certain that he absolutely did not want to sit there and whine to Sohan about his stupid problem with Ottokar, spilling the whole, sad, pathetic story of his lifelong torment in front of an even bigger audience. Hadn't he already been made a fool of enough?

"Thank you, but I'm afraid I will have to refuse the offer after all. There are some matters I need to attend."

"What?" Marcellette's face fell. "What

matters—"

"Pardon me, please," Amador said, and all but fled down the first turn he came to, barely noticing the bodyguards keeping pace, fleeing Marcellette calling after him.

He could only endure so much in one day, and the pond had been enough humiliation to last him the whole year. The very last thing his day needed was the abject pity that would fill Sohan's face as he listened to a recounting of the latest encounter with Ottokar.

What did it say about Amador that he could not get rid of the man who pursued him for the thrill of torment and rush of power, but could not get one person in several kingdoms to even consider him a marriage prospect? Why couldn't someone chase him with roses and gifts, eager to shower him in love and affection? Why was his most ardent pursuer a mean-hearted bully?

Back in his room, Amador changed out of his finer garments and into clothes more suited to long hours in a library, more relaxed in fit, sedate colors with little trim or decoration, the kind of clothes he could afford to have covered in ink and dust and other hazards that came with combing a library for hours on end.

Because he might not know a single damned thing about putting his own life in order, but he knew taxes and all the other boring rules and regulations that ran a country, and he suspected that might be the key to bridging the divide between a stubborn noblewoman and an even more stubborn royal guard.

First, though, he would need to do some research. *This* he was good at. *This* he could do.

Feeling somewhat heartened, if lonelier than ever, Amador headed out in search of the palace library.

The Library

Amador spent three days in the library doing research, starting with Pelletier, pulling out one book after another to learn the land and lineage in as much detail as the library could provide.

It was indeed a shockingly impressive territory for a baron. That was just as it was, not including all the *potential* it had, which was probably what truly drew all the councilors. Honestly, he was surprised only that they weren't fighting more viciously over it.

When he had the basics of Pelletier roughed out, he turned to his greatest strength, the place he was likeliest to find a weakness he could exploit: taxes. People like Lipovsky always either shamelessly avoided paying taxes, or left the problem entirely in the hands of whatever clerk or clerks they hired. In either case, something was always amiss.

Thankfully, like back home, tax records here were compiled and stored in the library. Unfortunately, they were kept in a restricted area. Well, only one way to learn what he would need to gain access. Approaching the main desk, Amador bowed his head in greeting to the librarian there. "Good afternoon, mistress. I wanted to know what is entailed in gaining access to the restricted areas."

The woman's cheeks flushed as she gave a small laugh. "Oh, His Majesty gave orders you were to have access to whatever you like, Your Highness."

Amador opened his mouth, then closed it. "He did?"

Tittering, the woman slid a key across the desk. "Yes, Your Highness. Did you not know? He issued a statement across the palace that you were to be treated as his personal guest. Keep that key as long as you're here, or until you'll no longer be needing it."

"I, uh, see. Thank you very much."

Utterly bemused, Amador retreated to the restricted section, where it didn't take him long to locate the tax records for the Pelletier Estate and Lipovsky's personal taxes. Carrying the enormous, heavy ledgers to the table he'd commandeered, he fetched his writing case and set out paper, pens, and various colors of ink.

By the third day, he was ready for the final stage. With ledgers on one side, and tax law books on the other, Amador set to work on gathering information and formulating a plan.

Taxes, always taxes. It didn't matter who they were, how powerful, how wealthy, there was always a flaw or weakness to be found in the taxes.

In Lipovsky's case, they were in arrears, though it looked like that was due to simple negligence rather than willful greed. He was also set to take a significant blow if the Filandra Amendment passed with the requirement that all dodged taxes be paid, which seemed the likeliest outcome, despite the efforts of various nobles, merchants, and robber barons.

Amador's stomach growled, but he ignored it, far more interested in pulling a fresh sheet of paper close and mapping out the rough details of his idea. He would need to hire someone to draft the actual contract, but that shouldn't be difficult. Notaries shouldn't be difficult either. No, the hardest part would be securing an appointment with Lipovsky, but Amador already had thoughts…

A sudden ruckus from the main section of the library broke his concentration. Curiosity piqued, Amador pushed away from the table and strode off between two looming stacks to see what the fuss was all about. His bodyguards remained where they were, which honestly in retrospect should have tipped him off.

In the center of the main space, surrounded by bodyguards, clerks, and librarians, was Sohan. His smile as he spoke with the head librarian made Amador's stomach flip, and he didn't think he was the only one who thought it lit up the room.

Amador couldn't see his beautiful eyes from here, alas, but there was still plenty to admire. Plenty to remember, like how it felt to be held, to feel safe. He could only imagine how it felt to be held like he was *wanted*.

He pushed the futile thought away before it could hurt him. He'd traveled the world in search of a prince or princess who would marry him. Not a single one had even come close. If he couldn't catch a prince, why in the world would he be able to catch a king?

Turning away, Amador retreated to the comforting familiarity of his books and papers, writing out a rough draft of the contract he wanted drawn up, pausing here and there to double check one detail or another.

He'd just managed to start on the third paragraph of what would likely be twelve when he heard footsteps, his bodyguards saying, "Your Majesty."

Amador's head snapped up, and then he pushed to his feet to bow over the mess scattered across his table. "Good…um, evening? Your Majesty."

Sohan chuckled as he came around the table. "Good evening, indeed. Have you really spent the last three days in here? I am told you arrive in the morning and leave in the evening."

"Yes?" Amador blinked, looked at the table, then back at Sohan, desperately trying not to stare. He really was so ridiculously beautiful, with the same flawless skin as his brother save for a thin scar that ran along the right side of his face from his temple to the back of his jaw, cutting a line through his close-cropped beard. His hair was curly, or tried to be, pulled back ruthlessly to stay out of his way but threatening to spring free at any moment.

If Amador were a glutton for punishment, he might wonder what that beard would feel like against his skin, or imagine those full, soft looking lips against his. He preferred not to torment himself though, especially not with someone so out of reach, so he didn't contemplate any such thing.

Sohan clucked. "Have you had anything to eat today?"

"Breakfast, I think?" Why in the world

did *the king* care if he'd eaten?

That got him a faintly reprimanding look. "I see. What are you working on so avidly?" He smiled faintly as he looked over the table. "Somehow I'm not surprised taxes are involved."

Amador's cheeks burned, but there was no point in pretending the obvious wasn't true. "I was curious about Lord Lipovsky's holdings."

"Oh? What provoked your curiosity?"

Amador would rather throw himself back into that stupid pond than admit he was attempting to play matchmaker for people he barely knew. He could only imagine how hard Sohan would laugh, dismiss his efforts, wonder why he wasn't doing something worthy of his time and skill. Or any of the hundred other things people said to him. "His reticence, all the upheaval with the Filandra Amendment, that sort of thing. Nothing special. I am sorry if I'm causing trouble for anyone or—"

Sohan held up a hand, stopping the apology, and then offered the hand palm up.

Heart thudding in his ears, Amador placed his own it, and his heart stopped completely when Sohan covered it with his other hand.

"No need to apologize, please. I wanted to make certain only that you were not being troubled, especially since I thought you'd join us for drinks after the council meeting, and instead you vanished entirely. Lady Marcellette said only that you were abruptly unable to come."

"Yes, I apologize," Amador said, painfully aware of Sohan's touch, struggling not to stare at their hands, into his beautiful eyes like a nitwit. "I seem to do nothing but cause you trouble and bother."

Sohan frowned. "Not at all. I am the one who is sorry that your time in my home so far has been so fraught. I promise once that little cretin has finished his business here, he will be sent on his way and not allowed back."

All the pleasure Amador had been taking in Sohan's presence withered. He hadn't thought anything could be worse than Ottokar's cruel disdain, his delight in Amador's misery, but Sohan's pity was *infinitely* worse. He didn't want Sohan pitying him, feeling sorry for him, he wanted Sohan to *see* him.

Withdrawing his hand, immediately missing Sohan's warm touch, Amador said, "You do not need to worry about me, Your Majesty. I'm used to dealing with him, and he is *my* problem. There are far more important things that require your attention. I am sorry that I have pulled you away from them."

Sohan stared at him, mouth pressed

together, brows drawn down. In the end, though, he only sighed and said, "All that happens within my home is my concern, but I can see that bringing the matter up distresses you, so I shall not continue to do so. Please do take care of yourself, Your Highness. I would not have you come to any sort of harm, big or small. Good evening, and sleep well when you find your bed."

Then he was gone, leaving only the winter-forest scent of his cologne behind, and an ache in Amador's heart.

He returned stiffly to his table, but it took several minutes of staring blankly before he was able to get his mind working again, to restore his focus to books and papers, taxes and contracts. Helping other people, because he had never been very good at helping himself.

Picking up his pen in a hand that still felt warm from Sohan's touch, he resumed drafting the contract.

Somewhere in the middle of paragraph five, a polite cough drew his attention. Amador looked up and stared blankly at the servant standing in front of him holding a silver tray near to overladen with food. "Prince Amador?"

"Yes, that's me."

The servant smiled. "I've brought a late repast for you as requested by His Majesty.

Where should I set it? I would hate to accidentally ruin something you're working on."

"Oh, um, I'll clear off—"

Before he could even stand, though, one of the bodyguards surged forward to clear off one half of the table, neatly and carefully stacking Amador's work on either the other half of the table or unused chairs.

"Thank you," Amador told her, and then thanked the servant as well as he set the tray down and bowed before slipping away.

Sohan had sent him food? Why? More pity? Did he think Amador that helpless?

No, none of that made sense. Sohan hadn't gotten angry when Amador crashed into him, and he'd helped Amador out of the pond himself rather than sending one of the bodyguards who'd been right there with him. Sohan was being polite, or kind, or both.

Stifling a sigh, at life but mostly himself, Amador set to work on his meal, stomach growling as it finally got what it had been complaining about over the past few hours.

When he was full, he kept what remained of the wine as he returned to work, stretching with a long groan before reclaiming his seat.

By the time he was forced to stop for the night, exhaustion and soreness finally winning out, he had the whole plan not just roughed out, but firmed up. All he needed was to have the paperwork officially drawn up and schedule an appointment with Lipovsky.

Thankfully, those were the easy parts. For better and worse, people rarely told a prince no. If only the Ottokars of the world listened when they *were* told no.

In his room, a bath was waiting, still steaming, by the fire that had been laid. "Bibiana, your timing is impeccable."

She laughed, looking up briefly from the jacket she was embroidering. "Wasn't me, though I was waiting for you to return so I could order the bath. This arrived just a few minutes before you did. I assumed you'd sent someone else with the order so it would be waiting."

"No…" Amador said softly, mind spinning with too many emotions to sort. Sending him food was one thing, but surely Sohan wasn't also responsible for the bath? That seemed far too much for simple kindness, even for pity. No, much more likely one of the librarians had said something to a servant, and something had gotten mixed up or misunderstood. "I was in the library all day again, must have been someone there, somehow. Suppose it doesn't matter. Soledad—"

"Sir?" Soledad asked, standing from the

desk where he'd been sorting through what looked like correspondence.

"Why are you working so late?"

"I wanted to run some errands in town, so I was trying to get a bit ahead on the correspondence now."

"Ah. Actually, if you're going to be in town, you can do your errands on duty if you'll also take this and get it properly drawn up for me, and locate some notaries that I'll need as soon as the contract is ready." He could easily have it all taken care of there in the palace, but if he did that the gossip would spread before dinner. "If you can also get me an estimate on when I will have it in hand, schedule an appointment with Lord Lipovsky that same day. That's when we'll need the notaries." He'd also need witnesses, but he'd sort that out later.

"Of course, Your Highness."

"Thank you, I appreciate it." Leaving Soledad to his work, he stripped off his clothes for Bibiana to take away and settled into the hot bath with a groan.

"Would you like your usual soaps, Highness, or one of the new ones?"

Amador's eyes snapped open. "New ones? What new ones?"

Bibiana turned and grabbed something behind her, presenting a beautiful blue wicker basket filled with soaps, lotions, creams, and more. Even a bottle of perfume, if he wasn't mistaken.

"Is this… meant for me?"

She eyed him like she was concerned he was losing his mind but couldn't find a polite way to suggest that. "Who else would it be meant for? It came along with the bath."

Someone, somewhere, was supremely confused and frustrated that their gift had gone—

"Oh, mercy me, there's a note," Bibiana said. "I'm so sorry, Your Highness." She pulled it out, set it aside, and offered a cloth for Amador to dry his hands.

Taking the note, Amador stared at it for a moment, not sure what to make of his name across the front in a beautiful script in gold ink on green paper.

Oh, gods, *ink*. "Bibiana, how much ink is on my face?"

Bibiana replied gently, "More than Your Highness would actually care to know."

Amador groaned as he covered his face with one hand. No wonder Sohan had felt so sorry for him: harassed into panicked flight by Ottokar, pushed into a pond, hiding in a library, and covered in ink stains. This was why he couldn't get a single person to marry him. He wouldn't want to marry a hopeless twit, either.

Breaking the gold wax seal on the

envelope, he pulled out the single small sheet of paper within and unfolded it.

I hope the sunrise brings a better day. Please take care of yourself. ~S

Amador's face went hot, and Bibiana barely caught the slip of paper before it fell into the tub.

S. He only knew one S that could do something like this in the middle of the night on the spur of the moment.

Bibiana seemed faintly amused, though her face gave nothing away, as she asked. "One of the new soaps, then, Your Highness?"

"Um, yes, I suppose so," Amador replied. One didn't exactly refuse a gift from a king. He just wished he knew *why* Sohan was being so nice.

He didn't dare hope the answer was the one he most wanted to hear.

Never mind he'd only been here a few days. Bit much to be getting so completely flustered by one person.

Even if that one person felt safe. Comforting. Seemed kind, gentle. Showed all signs of being a good leader and not an unbending tyrant.

If only Amador didn't somehow manage to make a complete and utter cake of himself every single time they crossed paths. Dinner and a bath. The things a mother—well, a good mother—made certain her child got.

Climbing out of the bath once he'd finished, Amador dried off leisurely, enjoying the smell of the soap he'd used, sweet orange and basil with a touch of frankincense. The basket of items caught his eye, and he couldn't resist poking through it more, setting aside a lotion that matched the soap he'd just used.

As he'd thought earlier, there was indeed a bottle of perfume. There was no maker's mark on it, but there didn't need to be: the pale lavender glass with a soft opalescent sheen was tell enough. House Vérène, one of the finest perfumeries in the world. Some would argue *the* finest.

Removing the stopper, he breathed in the scent that washed over him. Orange again, this time orange blossoms with a bare hint of bitter orange, with notes of pear, oakmoss, and coriander. It was an absolutely stunning scent, fresh and delicately pretty.

It was a strangely extravagant gift for someone Sohan was simply worried about like a mother over a child that kept running into or falling down things. He had apparently told everyone Amador was to be treated as his guest, though, and nobody who did things at the king's command did them by halves. So whoever had assembled the basket at Sohan's behest had probably simply erred on being thorough.

Replacing the stopper, he took the

lotion and the perfume to his vanity, then headed for the bed—and stopped as a knock came at the door.

Soledad rose from the desk to go answer it and returned with a note.

Amador's heart sped up—and dropped as he saw the small slip of white paper that was nothing like the green paper from before.

"You seem popular tonight, Your Highness," Soledad replied with a smile as he handed the note off.

"Haha," Amador replied absently as he opened the note.

You have ignored me for three nights, and I shan't tolerate further. Meet me in the garden immediately, or I will make you regret it! Marcellette

Amador laughed. He'd been so wrapped up in his plans, he'd completely forgotten she'd promised to show him 'something interesting' in the blue garden. "I've an appointment with a friend that I've neglected these past few days. Bibiana, would you fetch me something simple and plain?"

"Of course." She bustled off to the dressing room and was back in a moment.

Once he was dressed, Amador said, "You two go on to bed. I'll see you in the morning, or afternoon, even. After this long night, I doubt I'll be waking early."

"Yes, Your Highness."

After they'd gone, Amador tucked the note into his pocket and headed out to see interesting things in a garden.

Rendezvous

It took him a couple of tries, but he finally found the section labeled Blue Garden, and crept through the archway. Convincing his bodyguards to remain behind, and where they wouldn't be seen, took a good deal more work, but when he explained who he was meeting and why, they finally relented.

"Psst! Here! No, the cherry trees!"

Like he could tell one trees from another when it was so dark. He was lucky he hadn't dumped himself in another pond. He finally caught sight of a madly waving fan and followed it and Marcellette's imperious summons to a pair of cheery trees fronted by shrubs that came up to his hips. "If your Vladlena catches us huddling together in the bushes…"

Marcellette laughed. "She'll demand to know what mischief I'm up to now and why

I'm dragging poor innocent you into it. She has no room to talk, though, because she's even more involved in this particular mischief than I am. I think we're close to midnight now, shouldn't be long."

"I am most intrigued," Amador replied, and lapsed into silence.

True to Marcellette's pronouncement, they didn't wait long.

Two figures crept into the garden, speaking quietly, but their words carrying anyway. "Why do you keep doing this if you're never going to say anything? I'm telling you, if you just told him—"

"Not this again," Léonce said. "Stop it, please. I'll say something… eventually."

Vladlena snorted. "I don't know why you're so scared. I *promise* you that you'll get exactly the reaction you're hoping for. You'd have already gotten it if His Highness ever managed to stay awake to catch you, which clearly he does not."

"He always falls asleep reading or writing," Léonce muttered, then added, "I'm a gardener. He's a prince. Even if he didn't care about that, the entire rest of the palace would, including his brother *the king*. Now can we stop having this conversation for the thousandth time and get on with it?"

"Yes, Your Highness," Vladlena replied.

"You're so funny."

They stopped on the far side of the garden… below the balcony of a square turret. "Nazaire's chambers," Marcellette murmured, able to pitch her voice to not carry in a way Vladlena and Léonce were obviously trying to do but not really succeeding. "You smell nice, by the way. Sweet orange suits you marvelously, darling."

"Thank you. Sorry, I forgot."

Marcellette waved her closed fan in dismissal.

Across the garden, just visible in the lamplight Vladlena had brought along, she braced her hands for Léonce to step into and heaved him up onto her shoulders. From there, Léonce grasped two of the balustrades and pulled himself up, then deftly over, the balcony railing.

Once he was up, Vladlena tossed something into the air. Roses. An entire bouquet of roses, probably incredibly beautiful, given Léonce's skills.

Taking the roses, Léonce headed for the door of the balcony and pressed his ear to it. Satisfied with whatever he did or did not hear, he opened the door and slipped inside.

Amador almost laughed. Really? That's what he had to work with? This was going to be even easier than he thought. Helping Vladlena and Marcellette was vastly more complex. Once he finished with them, helping Léonce and Nazaire wouldn't take more than a few minutes work.

A few minutes passed, and then Léonce returned, climbing over the balcony and hanging down a moment before letting go and dropping deftly to the ground.

"Same time tomorrow?" Vladlena asked as she offered a hand and tugged him to his feet.

"Oh, be quiet," Léonce said without any heat. "You don't have to keep helping me."

"After seeing the way you nearly killed yourself doing it alone the first time? No, thanks. The last thing anybody in this palace wants is to find you lying next to your precious roses with a broken neck. That is definitely not the way to charm the prince of your dreams."

Léonce groaned and gave her a shove. "Have I mentioned lately that I hate you."

Vladlena snickered and threw an arm across his shoulders, moving the conversation to something involving the garden as they headed off.

Amador stood up, brushing leaves from his coat and wincing as his poor knees cracked. "You did not lie: that was interesting. Why haven't you said anything to Nazaire, if you know who his mysterious sweetheart is?"

"Because it's not my place, as much as I

would love to simplify everything. Léonce's fears are not unreasonable, for one. For two, I won't be the one making their choices for them."

"Not unreasonable? You really think His Majesty would be angry about the matter?"

Marcellette opened her beloved fan and flicked it impatiently. "Goodness, no. His Majesty is the deepest romantic in the palace. He was made king far too young and is more like a father to his siblings than a brother. He's never really gotten to live his own life, so he's vehement his siblings don't suffer the same. On the contrary, he'd defend the relationship to all comers. The rest of the court, though, would make Léonce's life miserable. It doesn't help that he's rejected tens of suitors, from amongst the court and the broader community. Turning down all of them and winding up with a gardener? Scandal of the century."

"People will have to get over it," Amador said.

"It won't help that neither Nazaire nor Léonce can provide children, and His Majesty is still single and childless. None of that would stop *me* from being with the person I love, but well…" She spread her hands and sighed. "It stops Léonce, and it stops Vladlena, and I can blame neither, even if I want to knock that stubborn woman upside her fool head."

Amador laughed. "Everything may yet work out. Don't give up hope quite yet."

"Never, darling, but you have me intrigued."

"I'm not telling you anything."

Marcellette's throaty laugh filled the hallway as they stepped into it. "Fine, fine. Have it your way. Will you be at breakfast? Certain parties have missed your company, and we hate to see him so forlorn."

"What? Who? I've dined in the hall once. How could anyone possibly miss me?"

Rolling her eyes, Marcellette said, "Men are hopeless. Goodnight, darling, see you in a few hours."

Amador groaned at the reminder there wouldn't be much sleep in his future, but he was soothed by the knowledge that his plans were coming together nicely. Bowing over Marcellette's hand in a playful imitation of a proper farewell, he said, "Goodnight, my lady. Should you need an escort to the garden some other night, you've only to ask."

"Sweet dreams, Your Highness," Marcellette replied, and with a laugh, headed down the hall toward her own rooms in the palace, wherever they were.

Amador yawned as he headed back to his own room and bid his bodyguards goodnight as he pushed into his room and closed the door. His fingers went to the buttons of his jacket, but he paused as movement caught his eye. "I thought you went—"

He stopped, hands dropping, blood going cold, as he realized it wasn't Bibiana by the fireplace.

It was Ottokar.

"What in the hells are you doing here?" Amador asked. "Get out."

"I've only come to talk, darling," Ottokar said. "Without those stupid thugs looming over me like they could actually lay a hand on me."

Amador's mind railed at him to leave, to call for help, but he was *tired* of running, of making everyone else fix his problems. Of appearing so fucking weak and pathetic. Ottokar was *his* problem, and *he* would handle it.

Stepping away from the door, he said, "There's nothing to talk about."

Ottokar made a derisive noise. "You are going to be mine, Amador, and it's time you accepted that. You've had your fun, traipsing around pretending like anyone else would ever marry you. It's long past time you ceased with all this nonsense and conceded defeat."

"I have no interest in a marriage that is described as *conceding defeat*."

Ottokar laughed in that way of his that cut to the bone, like a freezing wind or a stinging word from someone he'd thought a friend. "I mean, concede defeat that nobody else wants you. At all. You're the laughingstock of royalty, and it's time you admitted that and came home with me."

That struck closer to home that Amador liked admitting. How could he deny it, though? He'd traveled the world, seventeen kingdoms in all, and two empires, and the best he'd gained was a great many connections, several strong acquaintances, and maybe three people he would consider friends, though not close friends.

Nineteen places in all, and Portan made twenty. Nothing. Not a single relationship that could be described as serious, let alone strong enough to bring up marriage. One person and one person only had remained stubborn about marrying him this whole time.

Ottokar.

The only person who wanted him was cruel, malicious, and would probably leave him dead within a year after their marriage. Or would shunt him off somewhere to stay out of the way while Ottokar and their families benefited from sacrificing him like a lamb.

"I. Will. Not. Marry. You," he said, hating the tremble in his voice.

Ottokar laughed again and strode across the room toward like a snake about to strike.

Amador stayed right where he was,

though it took everything he had not to bolt.

Standing close enough to touch, the sour-sweet stench of his cologne stinging Amador's nose, Ottokar said, "Do you think here is going to be any different? Everywhere you go, nobody wants you." He smiled, sharp and mean. "The few stupid enough to consider it were easily put in their place."

"W-what? You. You didn't."

Ottokar laughed.

Amador wanted to *cry*. He was stupid. He was so fucking *stupid.* Ottokar had always shown up wherever he went, but it had never occurred to him that he'd been actively sabotaging Amador's efforts.

Despair turned to anger. "Get out."

"Not until—"

"I said get out!" Amador bellowed so loudly he hurt his throat. He *shoved*, sending Ottokar to the floor. "Get out! Get out! Get out!"

Ottokar surged to his feet, but Amador fled across the room to the fireplace, snatching up a vase on the mantel and lobbing it blindly.

It hit Ottokar square in the chest, shattering on impact and sending shards of porcelain flying, cutting.

"You little shit," Ottokar hissed as he wiped blood from his cheek. "I'm going to thrash you—"

The door slammed open, and the

bodyguards surged inside, swearing as they took in the scene. Before Ottokar could draw breath to tell him off, they were on him, pinning him to the floor, arms behind his back.

"I am a royal prince!" Ottokar snarled. "You will unhand me at once."

They bound his arms behind him with special rope they must carry on them and hauled him to his feet. As the broader of the two held him, the tall, imperious woman who'd told Ottokar off the last time they'd crossed paths said, "You were warned, Your Highness. You are a guest in this palace and remain solely at His Majesty's pleasure. You were warned that if you even dared to approach Prince Amador again that you would be removed. Given the severity of the current circumstances, you had best pray that His Majesty is in a forgiving mood."

Ottokar continued to snarl and threaten as the stockier guard dragged him away. Amador stared, bewildered and abruptly exhausted, until they were out of sight.

"Your Highness."

He turned his gaze to the guard who'd remained. "I'm sorry to have—"

"No, Your Highness," the woman said firmly, sinking to one knee, head bowed low. "We were charged with your protection, and to not clear your room before you entered it was a gross neglect of our duty. We beg your forgiveness."

"There's nothing to forgive, please. It never occurred to me he would do something this far out of line. I also should have had the sense to immediately call for you instead of being stubborn and dealing with him myself. Thank you for coming so quickly the moment you heard the ruckus."

"We will do better going forward, Your Highness."

"What's your name?" Amador asked. "I should have asked sooner, but I assumed..." That they were just doing a job foisted on them, that they wouldn't care if he knew their names or not.

"Tera, and my companion is Boris. I'll leave those who relieve us to introduce themselves. It has been our pleasure to serve, Your Highness, and I'm sorry again we failed so miserably."

"Please don't worry upon it. As long as I don't have to deal with him anymore, I'm content."

"You will not so much as see his face." Tera rose at his bidding, bowed, and strode from the room. He could hear her speaking to someone in the hallway as the door closed.

Scrubbing at his face, wishing this whole day was already a distant memory, Amador stripped out of his clothes and put his dressing robe back on. Pouring himself a drink, he sat by the fire to simply unwind. If he tried to go to sleep now, no matter how exhausted he was, he would toss and turn uselessly, or worse, fall into terrible nightmares.

When an urgent knock came at the door, he wasn't even surprised. Probably his bodyguards again. Heaving to his feet, Amador trudged to the door and opened it—and practically seized as he stared at Sohan. Of course. Really he should have expected it; his days weren't complete without Sohan arriving to bear full witness to his humiliation and misery.

"May I come in?" Sohan asked. "Please don't feel obligated to say yes, I am certain you've had more than enough people barging into your space for one night. I wanted only to ascertain personally that you were well." He looked back over his shoulders, a thundercloud falling over his face. "And to speak with your guards."

"Don't punish them," Amador blurted out.

Sohan's head snapped back to him, thundercloud easing slightly but still very much there. "What?"

Amador stepped back and motioned him inside, adding "please" when Sohan hesitated. Closing the door, he folded his arms, then let them drop, hands clenching and unclenching. "I don't want anyone punished or terminated because of me."

"They failed in their duty," Sohan said. "You could have been *killed*."

"It wasn't their fault! They've stood up for me flawlessly every time they've so much as caught a hint of Ottokar's vile cologne wafting down the hallway. In all the years I've been putting up with him, he's never once crossed the line into breaking into my room. How could they anticipate that if even I didn't?"

"They are bodyguards. It's their job—"

"To protect me from reasonable threats, not anticipate the behavior of someone as— As— As monstrous as Ottokar. Please, I know you're probably tired of me, tending to a guest like some child that can't take care of themselves. You certainly owe me no favors, but please, I am begging you, do not punish or terminate my bodyguards because of me, because of Ottokar."

Sohan stared at him, face drawn tight, eyes pensive. After a moment, he sighed, the tension bleeding from his shoulders. "As you wish. If they fail again, though, I will not be so lenient, not even for you." He stepped closer and offered his hand the same way he had in the library.

Heart pounding harder than ever,

Amador once more placed his in it, scarcely daring to breathe as Sohan covered it with his other hand. The gesture was a simple one, not even remarkable, and yet Amador would give everything he owned to make that touch last forever. When Ottokar was in the room, Amador felt like he was suffocating.

When Sohan was in the room, Amador felt like he could breathe properly for the first time in his life.

"I apologize that I have overstepped my bounds," Sohan replied. "I do not regard you as a child, not in the slightest. My parents died when I was quite young, and I have been parent and king most of my life, so I am afraid that I most often express myself by tending and managing those in my circle. My siblings have learned to tell me quite baldly to my face that I should shove it."

Amador scowled. "That seems rude and ungrateful."

Sohan laughed. "Overbearing is overbearing. I take no offense. I am sorry, though, that in my efforts to help I have only added to your discontent. I will have more care." He hesitated, a look of uncertainty passing like a shadow across his face. In the next beat it was gone, though, and he said, "I must depart for a couple of days, to attend a matter at the border. Nothing terrible, but it does require my presence. When I return, I would like to speak to you of something, if it pleases."

"Um, of course. Simply let me know what time is most convenient for you upon your return and I'll come."

"Thank you," Sohan said, the words gentle, but his eyes burning as he slowly withdrew his hands. "I hope you are able to sleep, and dream only of good things. Farewell, Your Highness. I'll see you in three days."

"T-three days," Amador said, and sat right down on the floor as the door closed behind Sohan, holding his hands to his chest in an effort to calm his thundering heartbeat.

What in the world was going on? Why did Sohan want to speak with him? Why not just say it *now*, instead of making him suffer for three days?

Too much. This whole day had been far too much.

Pushing to his feet, Amador locked the door, put out the lights and stoked the fire, and then finally headed to bed. It was only as he reached it and stripped off his robe though that he realized he'd just been speaking to Sohan alone in his room while wearing only a dressing robe. Of course he had.

Exhausted beyond all reason, Amador climbed into bed and mercifully fell quickly asleep.

The Baron's Heir

It took two days for the paperwork to be ready, and nearly as long to secure an appointment with Lipovsky, who seemed to be avoiding everyone, which was fair, as he probably felt like a fish surrounded by hungry sharks.

After breakfast with Nazaire and Marcellette, he headed for the office Nazaire had given to him to borrow as long as he liked, where Soledad already waited with the lawyer and notaries. "Stay, please," Amador said as his bodyguards started to take up position in the hallway like usual. "I would like you to be present, so you can report on details to His Majesty should it be necessary."

The taller of the two women protecting him today frowned. "Do you anticipate trouble, Your Highness?"

"No, not at all. Maybe some colorful

swearing at worst. I simply want witnesses to all this for the sake of thoroughness."

"As you wish, Highness."

"Thank you." Amador took his seat, and had only just settled when a knock came at the door. Soledad rose to answer it, and Lipovsky entered with his own secretary. His bushy brows were drawn down in a sharp V, mouth flat. "Your Highness, I am here as requested."

"I appreciate you coming, Baron, and on such short notice," Amador replied, motioning for them to sit on the opposite side of the table. "I promise this will be worth your time and effort."

Lipovsky said nothing, as they all knew very well that a lowly baron was in no position to brush off or threaten a prince, even a foreign one. "My pleasure to serve."

"It's in fact I that am here to help you." Amador gave a bare nod of his head, and next to him the lawyer laid out the reports Amador had put together. "Your estate is heavily in debt from mismanaged taxes. I suspect part of the reason you've been putting off declaring an heir is that the problem would become public knowledge when so far you've managed to keep it quiet."

"How did *you* learn of it? You've been here barely more than a week. This has nothing to do with you, Your Highness."

Amador spread the papers out. "That is

for me to decide. Now, then, your problem compounds with the enacting of the Filandra Amendment, since many of the businesses located in your territory will take significant strikes from it." He pushed one of the pages forward. "I'm sure you've done the numbers yourself, but for the sake of thoroughness, this is the total amount your territory will owe. That is not an amount you will be able to cover, and most of the businesses will close."

"I'm aware of the problems," Lipovsky said icily. "I don't need some foreign prince trotting in to explain them to me."

"No, I suppose you don't, but you do need someone to provide the funds you require to come out of this mess. I also suggest you hire better accountants going forward, but we can discuss that later. Let's come to the point: I will pay your debt in full and grant you a generous surplus besides. If properly managed, the money will be more than capable of bringing your territory back up to flourishing."

Lipovsky's eyes widened, then narrowed. "What is your price?"

"Your heir of course," Amador replied. "You will name the person of my choosing as your heir."

"Naturally. What in the world could my territory possibly offer you?" Lipovsky asked, almost vibrating in place, anger and despair warring in his eyes.

Amador motioned to the lawyer again, who slid the contract across the table. "Nothing. Your territory doesn't interest me. What I want, the only thing I want, is for you to name Sergeant Vladlena Fosse your heir."

Lipovsky jolted as though brutally backhanded. "Her? To what end?"

"Doing the right thing is end enough."

Lipovsky laughed. "The right thing? Lifting up a whore's daughter?"

"Your daughter," Amador said, and Lipovsky recoiled from the heat in his voice.

"What's your real motive?"

"Read the contract. Come to your own conclusions."

"I will," Lipovsky bit out.

"It's sound," Lipovsky's lawyer said, regarding Amador and then his lawyer pensively. "Exquisite work, honestly."

Amador's lawyer smiled crookedly. "I would love to take credit, because it is most excellent work, but I just did the finishing. His Highness drafted it."

"You would make an excellent lawyer, Your Highness."

Lipovsky shifted impatiently, clearly fighting an urge to roll his eyes. "If we're quite finished fawning…"

"It's a sound contract," Lipovsky's lawyer said, a slight hint of reprimand in his tone. "Everything he promised, and indeed all he wants in return is that Sergeant Fosse is named your heir—and remains your heir, not to be removed by any means. Should you renege and dismiss her as your heir, the consequences are severe."

Fierce brows furrowed again, Lipovsky pulled the contract close and read it for himself, leaving the room in a long, heavy silence. The two lawyers seemed to have some silent exchange that was not in Lipovsky's favor, but Amador remained out of it. He was pushing enough as it was—pushing too far, arguably, but no one else had been trying to solve the problems, and he could make a lot of people happier in one move. Happier, more stable, less worried and miserable.

"I can find no flaw," Lipovsky said stiffly, pushing the contract away. "You do indeed seem to want nothing for yourself, Your Highness, though I wonder what is going on in places I cannot see."

"Nothing. You will have to learn that for yourself, though. If you are amenable, then, we shall get to the signing?"

"Witnesses?" Lipovsky's lawyer asked.

Amador motioned to his bodyguards. "If you're willing?"

"As it pleases you, Your Highness."

Lipovsky signed first, then Amador, then the witnesses. The notaries came last, making everything official and final. One copy went to Lipovsky, one to Amador, a third that Amador set aside, and the official papers to his own lawyer to be properly filed.

Amador rose, tucking his copy and the spare into his jacket. "Once I know that you've officially made Vladlena your heir, I will pay the debts, send you proof, and have the additional deposited in your bank of choice. Simply send me the information."

"Yes, Your Highness," Lipovsky said as he stood and bowed. There was the barest hesitation, and then he added gruffly, "Thank you, Your Highness. You've helped me immensely, and spared me having to contend with the vultures of the council. You are astute, and smart, and appear to know tax law better than every clerk I've ever hired."

The lawyers laughed as they shook hands before bowing to Amador. "Indeed, Your Highness. If you ever grow weary of royal life, you'd find a solid career in tax law, which you probably know full well."

"I have heard that one or twice, but my interest in largely academic, which I realize is a luxury. Thank you all for your assistance in this matter, especially considering how quickly I wanted it done."

His lawyer bowed again. "It's been our honor to be of service, Your Highness."

They all filed out of the room, leaving

Amador alone with his bodyguards and Soledad.

"That went very well, Your Highness," Soledad said. "You do have a knack for these things."

Amador waved the words aside. "It's not hard to sit around making offers people can't really refuse when you're a royal prince. Thank you for the help, Soledad. I'd be lost without your impeccable skill. I am deeply grateful to you two as well," he added, turning to the bodyguards. Pulling out the spare copy he'd retained, he offered it to the nearest of them. "Would you see that is given to His Majesty's office, so he can peruse at his leisure when he returns?"

"Of course, Your Highness."

"I appreciate it. Now, then, on to the bank to finalize those arrangements." He headed to his room first, to change into suitable clothes for going out, and then they were off into the city.

At the bank, clerks came rushing up to him immediately, escorting him off to a lush office that overlooked the ocean, offering first cocktails and then tea when he refused the alcohol. "Your Highness, it's such an honor to meet you," greeted the official who sat next to him, leaving the remaining two clerks to hover. "We of course got your missive that you would be visiting Portan, but I admit we did not expect the pleasure of properly meeting you."

"I try always to meet those I do any manner of business with," Amador replied. "You will be handling my finances, after all. I should know your faces. I had planned for a less dramatic meeting than this, but I'm grateful for all you've done, and so quickly."

"It's our pleasure, Your Highness. We have readied all the funds, though we're still readying the various individual debts. There's many of them to process, and we want to be absolutely certain all the funds go where they are intended. We will bring you copies of all the paperwork as we gather it. The funds to go to Baron Lipovsky are ready to be transferred. They require only the destination and your final authorization."

Amador nodded. "We should have it soon. I do not anticipate our good baron will dally in taking action. You'll likely have everything outstanding by tomorrow, day after at the latest. How do more mundane matters proceed?"

"Flawlessly, Your Highness. If I might say, it helps immensely that all your paperwork was perfectly in order. That is…less common than one might suspect." The official cleared his throat, then pushed some papers over to Amador. "The receipts are here, and copies of our records as requested. Some of the funds will not reach their final destinations for a few more days, but we do not anticipate trouble. There is always a risk of highway robbers, but we pay well for protection."

"I appreciate it. Everything looks in order to me," Amador said, and signed off on the papers after reading them.

As they rose, the official asked, "Is there anything else I can do for you today, Highness?"

"I'd like to withdraw some funds for shopping and general use. Say ten thousand? Half to remain with me, the rest to be sent on to my rooms in the palace."

"Of course, Your Highness." The official snapped his fingers at the hovering clerks, and in short order Amador had his funds.

The official walked him through the bank and to the door, where he hesitated. "If you will pardon me a moment of personal comment, Your Highness…?"

Amador blinked. "Yes, by all means."

"I wanted to express my thanks for all that you do."

"All that I do?"

The official smiled. "My wife is from Tesh. She came here after she finished her schooling—schooling she would never have been able to afford on her own. She attended on one of your scholarships. We'd never have met if not for the assistance you provide."

Amador broke into a wide smile. "Oh, I'm so happy to hear that! I confess I do little beyond provide the funds. The real work is done by other people, each of them marvelous at their job."

"The money makes all the difference, but I assure you my wife has thanked them as well. I simply saw an opportunity to thank you personally and did not want to miss it. Should you have further need of us, you've only to write or send for us."

"Thank you, and have a good rest of the day."

Outside, Amador let out a long, soft sigh, smiling faintly. So far, this day was going well. He half expected Ottokar to come around the corner any moment.

"You offer scholarships, Your Highness?" one of his bodyguards, Reta, asked.

"Hmm? Oh, yes. Well, it's a charity to provide schooling for the 'less fortunate,' though I always hated that phrase. It awards approximately three hundred scholarships a year. I'm told competition for them is quite fierce. All the way in Portan, and I manage to encounter a winner." He laughed. "All right, if you don't mind, I would like to do a bit of shopping before returning to the palace."

"We serve at your pleasure, Your Highness."

He smiled and thanked them with a nod. "Well, it wouldn't do to keep you out past shift change."

Reaching the carriage, he gave the driver the places to visit, leaving it to him to choose whatever order made the most sense.

The first stop was to select fabric for new clothes, colors and patterns that would hold him in good stead no matter where he was, as he traveled far too much to ever keep up with the latest fashion. Once those were done and sent on to a tailor that Nazaire had recommended to visit later in the week, they traveled to the next stop, where he probably spent far too much time and effort selecting new stationery, pens, and inks, as his current set had not endured well through all his traveling.

Probably a silly thing to buy if he wound up running away after all. Then again, good stationery went far when seeking housing, a job, and other such things. Things he'd never had to do before, so he'd need every advantage he could get.

He had the feeling his future rested on the conversation Sohan wanted to have, but despite hours of worrying himself to death over the matter, Amador still had no idea what Sohan would need to speak with him about.

The only thing he'd accomplished here so far was technically still in progress, and he wouldn't know until tomorrow if his plan for tonight truly worked.

Neither of his little bits of mischief really amounted to much, not enough that a king would think he was useful enough to keep around.

His hands, resting on his thighs, curled inward as the memory of Sohan's gentle touch rose up. What? What could Sohan possibly want to speak with him about that had to wait three long, torturous days? Possibly longer, if he was delayed.

Amador drew a deep breath and let it out slowly. There was nothing he could do but wait. Thankfully, there wasn't much of that left to do, and he'd be busy part of tonight, which would make the time go all the faster.

The final stop of the day was a jewelry store. For each of his bodyguards he selected a pair of earrings, small, bejeweled hoops that would more than suit a fine occasion, small enough to wear even while working if they chose, but more remarkable than simple studs.

Next was an infinitely more difficult task: selecting a thank you gift for Sohan. No gift really seemed adequate for a man who'd done so much for him, for no reason at all. Leaving aside that Sohan was king and could buy and have practically anything, he received gifts daily for tens, if not hundreds, of reasons. There would be an entire team who did nothing but manage the influx of gifts that the throne received, putting them to use where most suitable or needed, with almost none of them actually going to Sohan.

So what could he possibly gift that would stand out from the deluge? Nothing, really, but he finally settled on a line bracelet of moss green peridot set in yellow gold. Simple, classic, and the exact color of Sohan's eyes. Also reminiscent of a certain stupid pond, for better and worse.

"All right," he said as he left the jewelry store. "Let's go home, shall we?"

"Yes, Your Highness!" his servants and bodyguards chorused, and with a smile, Amador climbed into the carriage.

The Prince's Suitor

"You! You, you, *you!*"

Amador froze, until he registered Marcellette's voice, at which point he laughed as he turned to face the figure barreling toward him in a billowy pink dress, fan out and ready for thwacking or poking or both. "Me?"

"You!" Marcellette said, then broke into a smile before throwing herself at Amador and hugging him tightly.

Barely keeping them upright, Amador managed an 'oof,' but didn't get further as Marcellette drew back enough to kiss each of his cheeks before hugging him tightly again.

"I can't breathe," Amador gasped out.

Giggling, Marcellette let him go and backed up a couple of steps. "How did you do it?"

"So I take it Lipovsky has announced his decision?" Amador asked. "He worked even faster than I thought he would."

Marcellette held out her right hand, where a large blue diamond caught the fading sunlight and cast rainbows across the wall. "He has indeed, and his lovely, beautiful, perfect heir has *finally* accepted my offer of marriage, which just about made Lipovsky pass out."

Amador took her hand and dusted a kiss to her knuckles. "Congratulations on your engagement, my lady."

"You are a scheming schemer." Marcellette fluttered her fan and hooked her arm through his. "You will join me for tea and tell me *exactly* what you did to make him cooperate where no one else could. You've not been here even two weeks! I do believe, sir, that you have out-mischiefed me. I would be most cross, but you have given me the only thing in the world that I want, and for that I will forgive you anything and everything."

"All I did was throw money at the problem," Amador replied, nearly panting to keep pace with her.

They finally came to a stop in a little parlor overlooking a garden he hadn't seen yet, a tea service for three being arranged by a couple of servants who paused briefly to bow as they saw him.

Before Amador could even catch his breath, the door opened and Vladlena strode in—not in uniform, but in dark blue breeches and a jacket in a lighter shade of blue, a diamond broach on one lapel, a diamond ring similar to Marcellette's on her finger.

She smiled as she saw him and tipped into a deep bow. "Your Highness, I do not know what you did to convince the Baron—err, my father, to acknowledge me and take me as heir, but I am eternally grateful. It's an honor to make your acquaintance properly. I've heard much of you from Prince Nazaire and Marci."

"The honor is mine," Amador replied as the servants faded off, and they took their seats. "I hadn't realized he would say anything about what compelled his decision."

"Not much, but the few things he did say, it wasn't hard to put together that he was talking about you," Marcellette replied as she poured tea and put a few slices of sandwich on her plate. "Tell me, tell me, tell me."

Amador laughed as he nibbled at a sandwich of his own. "Not much to tell. There are few problems in the world that money cannot solve. I offered him funds more than sufficient to save his drowning estate and bring it back to flourishing. My condition was our good sergeant here."

"You asked for Vladlena to be his heir? That's it?"

"Why does everyone keep asking that?

What could I possibly need from him? I just wanted to help a friend. Well, someone I consider a friend."

"We are most definitely friends, you silly man," Marcellette said, waving her fan about until Vladlena deftly snatched it from her and set it out of reach. Marcellette pouted. "Give that back."

"After I've finished my tea, so I don't get whacked while I'm drinking," Vladlena retorted. "Again."

Marcellette huffed. "It was *one* time, and frankly, you deserved it."

Vladlena rolled her eyes. "Incorrigible."

"Yet here you are choosing to be stuck with me," Marcellette said, smug and so happy all Amador could do was sit there smiling as he watched them.

"Maybe I just want to make off with your fortune and please my father," Vladlena said loftily.

Marcellette just giggled in that engaging way of hers and went back to her tea and sandwiches.

Vladlena turned her attention to Amador. "Truly, Your Highness, I cannot thank you enough. My father and I have never gotten on, for obvious reasons, but I think matters will improve greatly from here on. It certainly doesn't hurt that I have you for support, though no one is more surprised than me, and that I've landed the catch of the season."

"I just want to see my friends happy," Amador said softly. "It was an easy enough matter to resolve, as I said. All anybody ever wants is the freedom of choice, and while he probably did not feel he had any choice at the moment of signing, I suspect by now his lordship is realizing just how many choices he now has. I am happy to serve."

Marcellette smiled mischievously. "Happy to impress, too, I bet."

Amador gave her a puzzled look. "Who is there for me to impress?"

Not having her fan, Marcellette toyed with her teacup instead. "Hmm, let me think. Tall, handsome, beautiful green eyes, commanding presence, a tendency to be overprotective and managing, has not stopped asking questions about—oof. Stop that!"

"You stop that," Vladlena retorted.

Marcellette folded her arms across her chest. "I'm only speaking the truth."

"I am here simply as part of my tour before returning home to do as my parents bid me," Amador replied. Gods, was he that pathetically obvious, fawning over Sohan so openly? Here he thought he'd managed to keep his nonsense to himself.

"I still say that if your choice is between that pustulant toad Ottokar and being homeless, you should go with homeless," Marcellette said, setting her teacup down with a sharp clack. "Not that we'd ever let such a thing happen. The stories of all you've done in your travels grow and grow."

Amador gave them a puzzled look. "All I've done? I haven't done anything."

Vladlena returned the puzzled look with an incredulous one. "No? What about Princess Arlanda?"

"What about her?" Amador asked.

Marcellette stole back her fan and opened it with a snap. "Rumor has it you bought up her lover's debts and forgave them."

"Yes? Because they were really her father's debts, and it was stupid they couldn't marry because of a reason that was so trivial to me. Buying up debts is hardly remarkable."

"Hmm…" Marcellette said. "What about Prince Michael? Prince Rolf? Lord Demesne? Haddarow? Qwelling?"

Amador rolled his eyes. "I don't think helping people out here and there is anything remarkable. It's hardly difficult to look over tax documents, or loan money, or assist with a negotiation. I am royalty—we are supposed to do those things. His Majesty and Prince Nazaire do the same sorts of things every day."

"I don't think either one of them has traveled the world to do it, and never asked for a single thing in return," Vladlena said. "The stories really are remarkable."

"Why is everyone talking about me?" Amador muttered into his tea.

"Because a certain someone asked questions, which set off a ripple effect, and now you are the talk of the palace, darling," Marcellette said with entirely too much glee. "A charming little prince spreading good fortune wherever he goes."

Amador rolled his eyes again. "I think the stories have, as they so often do, gotten blown massively out of proportion." How charming and whatever else could he really be, when nobody ever thought he was worth keeping? He helped, he was thanked, he went on his way. His desperate bid to avoid the fate of marrying Ottokar had gotten him an overblown reputation for being a soft touch, and that was it.

"You're a darling," Marcellette said, practically cooing the words. "Someone should consider himself extremely fortunate you're still available."

"I don't think anyone cares where I'm available or not, except Ottokar. Could we talk about something else, please?"

Vladlena motioned sharply when Marcellette pouted and tried to protest. "Of course, I apologize we've made you uncomfortable."

"Yes, yes," Marcellette said. "So do you have any further plans here at Portan?"

At that, Amador smiled. "I may have some thoughts about tonight, if you care to accompany me to the garden again, milady."

Vladlena narrowed her eyes, staring first at Amador and then Marcellette. *"What* garden visit, you troublemakers?"

"Why, the one where we watch you assist a certain stubborn gardener sneak roses into a certain royal's chambers."

"Oh, for the love of—" Vladlena's head fell back as she groaned-sighed. "I should have known you were there! How did I never once think 'I should check the hedges for the mischief making love of my life'?"

Marcellette giggled into her fan. "Indeed, you should have. So we'll see you tonight, darling? I want to see what our clever, matchmaking prince here has come up with."

"Nothing even remotely impressive. Simplicity is the key. Now if you will excuse me, ladies, I must go hold up my end of the bargain with the good baron and attend a few other matters. Thank you for inviting me to tea."

Marcellette fluttered her fan. "Ta, darling. Until tonight."

"Until tonight," Amador replied dryly before bowing and departing.

Back in his room, he changed into

clothes more suitable for getting some work done and then settled at his desk, where the packages from the stationery shop waited. Unwrapping them, he put everything neatly away, lingering over the beautiful inks, a set of twenty, each one a different jewel-toned color. More than he strictly needed, but he absolutely did not care.

Once his desk was set, he opened the letter from Lipovsky that had been waiting for him as well, and sent it off with a letter of his own to the bank so the money could be transferred. After that he drafted a long letter to his parents detailing why he absolutely would not marry Ottokar, all that Ottokar had done to him over the years, emphasizing the recent events in Portan and how bad it looked for their respective families.

He doubted the letter would accomplish anything, but he believed in being thorough.

After that, he caught up on the correspondence that Soledad had set in a tidy pile for him. When all that was finally done a couple of hours later, he wrote out notes of thanks to his bodyguards and a short letter of thanks to Sohan, then carried them to the table where the gifts waited, neatly wrapped in silk kerchiefs, marked for him by Soledad. Affixing the notes, Amador summoned Edu to deliver them all, save for Sohan's gift, which he wanted to deliver personally.

His chores concluded, there was nothing else for him to do for the day, so he put out the card to signal he'd eat in his room that night and went to take a nap.

When he woke a few hours later, the room was quiet, no sound, save the scratch of pen on paper as Soledad worked at his desk, and the pop-crackle of the fire. "What time is it?"

"Just past eleven, Your Highness," Soledad replied, not pausing in his writing.

Amador jolted. "So late? How did I sleep so long?"

Bibiana clucked her tongue as she came out of the dressing room carrying a jacket she was slowly embroidering. "Mercy alive, Your Highness, you slept so long because you needed the rest. Don't think you've gotten proper sleep in an age, what with one thing and another."

Well, there was no denying that. "Did I miss anything important?"

He swore the two of them shared a sly look before Soledad replied, "No, Your Highness, though it might interest you to know that His Majesty returned about an hour or so ago. There's a missive for you on your desk. I would have woken you, but His Majesty gave strict instructions we weren't to do so, and…" He spread his hands, then went back to writing.

"It's fine." He'd have preferred to be woken up, but it hardly mattered in the end. No doubt Sohan had been busy since his return, anyway.

Climbing out of bed, Amador pulled his clothes back on and went to the desk, where another envelope made of that beautiful green paper waited, with his name once more written in gold.

Inside was paper of a lighter green, the writing in dark blue ink. Amador had expected to be given some date and time in the near future, perhaps a couple of days out at best. Instead, the missive said only, *Please come see whenever you have the time and feel so inclined. I'll be awake some hours yet. If not tonight, then please do come see me for breakfast.*

Amador swore softly. Everything in him screamed to go see Sohan *right now*, but there was no telling how long their conversation would take, and he did not want to disrupt his plans for the night, especially since Marcellette and Vladlena were already expecting him.

So he tucked the note in his jacket, along with the bracelet and letter of thanks, fixed his hair, and ate the food that was sitting on the table by the fire before dashing out, bound for the garden.

He was not remotely surprised his co-

conspirators were already there, and looking suspiciously flushed as he pushed through the shrubs. "Good evening," Amador said with a laugh. "Having fun?"

"Quite," Marcellette said primly as she fixed the sleeve of her gown and smoothed down her hair.

Looking entirely pleased with herself, Vladlena said, "I'll signal when it's safe for the two of you to come out of hiding. I don't suppose you're going to tell me what you're planning?"

"Unlucky to share your plans before you absolutely must," Amador said, just to see them pout and scowl.

"You two are a *terrible* combination, I would like to put that on record," Vladlena said, then kissed Marcellette quick and sweet before going to take her usual position in the garden.

Amador looked around for a suitable stick, which thankfully did not take long, then doused his lantern and settled behind the shrubs with Marcellette

Not a moment too soon, either, as Léonce came into view carrying a large bouquet of roses.

"Ready for another night of frustrating you and your beloved by confessing your love but not your identity?" Vladlena asked cheerfully.

"Oh, shut up," Léonce said lightly. "Just because everything has worked out for you doesn't mean it's ever going to work for the rest of us. I was actually thinking maybe I should give up." He sighed.

"I think you should give up the secrecy, not the adoration, but you don't listen to anyone but your own stupid, stubborn self." Vladlena held up a hand before Léonce could voice the retort that comment deserved. "Take it from an expert on the matter. If not for Prince Amador's machinations, I'd probably still be acting just as stubbornly as you. Don't be me."

Léonce shrugged irritably. "*You* came into a sudden title and fortune. *I'm* still just a gardener."

"I think it might surprise you how easily you could wind up royalty, Lee, but come on, we'll keep doing things your way. Up, up."

Gently setting the roses aside, Léonce climbed onto Vladlena's shoulders with practiced ease, then heaved himself onto the balcony. Vladlena tossed the roses, and then he was gone again, sneaking away into Nazaire's bedroom.

After a few moments, Vladlena turned and waved her arm. Amador and Marcellette hastened out of the shrubs and joined her. "So what's the plan, Your Highness?"

"Get me up there like you do him, and

then toss this after me," Amador said, handing over the stick, which was short and thick, not easily broken, especially while trying to keep quiet.

Vladlena stared at it blankly a moment and then she and Marcellette gaped at him. "You evil bastard," Marcellette said with absolute delight. "I love it!"

"Come on, we have to hurry," Amador said.

He wasn't anywhere near as smooth about the climb as Léonce, and it took him two tries, but he did finally scramble up, panting and gasping. Thankfully it was much easier to catch the stick, and then there was really only one important step left.

Striding up to the doors, he slid the stick through the handles. Perfect. He took a step back and then simply waited.

The wait wasn't long. Not more than a minute or so, and someone on the inside gave the doors a push. Stopped. Gave them a firmer push. Amador just caught someone swearing. Stepping close the door again, he pressed his ear to the glass and listened.

Restless movement. Softly muttered words of panic. Still too quiet. Léonce might not be able to get out the balcony doors, or sneak past the guards at the main door, but he could find a place to hide and wait for his chance to break out of the room. That wouldn't do.

Drawing a deep breath, silently begging Léonce's forgiveness for so much mischief, Amador pounded loudly on the door. There was much louder swearing happening as he pressed his ear to the door a second time, followed by a panicked prince jerking awake—and then gasping Léonce's name.

Withdrawing, Amador returned to the balcony railing and threw his arms up in a sign of victory. Down below, the other two cheered.

Now for the getting down part, which hadn't looked nearly so intimidating when he'd watched Léonce do it.

He landed with neither grace nor dignity, but no broken bones either, so he would take it.

"Well? Well?" Marcellette asked eagerly.

Amador laughed, lifting his hands. "I don't know much. I heard Nazaire say Léonce's name, so it's safe to say he was caught. I apologize, Vladlena, that Léonce will likely believe you were responsible for the door and knocking."

Vladlena laughed. "I was involved, even if I didn't do the important work."

"If you think I could have ever gotten up there on my own…" Amador said.

"Drinks! Drinks!" Marcellette cheered,

standing between them and linking her arms through theirs. "To the glass room! Allons-y!"

"Allons-y!" Amador and Vladlena echoed, and headed off through the garden, through the palace, to what proved to be an absolutely beautiful room, more like a gazebo combined with a balcony and the whole covered in colored glass, set to softly glinting in the moonlight.

Servants arrived shortly after they did with trays of sparkling wine and finger foods, looking faintly amused as they filed out again. Though Amador ached to go see Sohan, he was loathe to leave his friends, when he could not remember the last time he'd had friends who would invite him to something as silly and self-indulgent as midnight champagne.

As though summoned, a familiar laugh came from the doorway, and Amador turned to see Sohan watching them. "What do we have here?"

The King

Sohan was, for once, dressed rather plainly, in only a linen shirt that had no business fitting so snugly, breeches that were faded, especially at the knees, stockings and boots. He didn't even have a jacket, yet seemed not to feel the chill in the air.

"Your Majesty," Marcellette said. "We are celebrating Prince Amador's marvelousness."

"We are not!" Amador hissed, face burning as he scowled at her. "Stop that right now!"

"Good luck with that," Vladlena said with a snort.

Marcellette looked not remotely repentant. "My engagement, then, that would not have happened without you because I am marrying the most stubborn-headed woman in the world."

Vladlena gave her a look. "You don't get to make that accusation."

Clearly amused, Sohan stepped further into the room and accepted the champagne that Marcellette thrust at him. "Congratulations, Lady Marcellette, Lady Vladlena, and on your recent appointment as Lord Lipovsky's heir. However did you talk him around?"

"That is the doing of our darling Amador!" Marcellette said, and before Amador could stop her, launched into the tale of all he'd done, leaving Amador no choice but to flesh out details as needed.

Unsurprisingly, that led into an explanation of what exactly had inspired the midnight champagne.

Sohan smiled and once again, Amador found his hand enveloped in both of Sohan's. "You seem much happier than when I left. I'm glad. I did not mean to interrupt your time with your friends, though."

"You didn't. I was going to drink a couple of glasses and then come see you, if you were still awake."

"Nonsense, nonsense," Sohan replied. "I will see you tomorrow, maybe at breakfast, after I've had a conversation with my brother that clearly should have happened sooner. Thank you for doing so much for us, little more than strangers to you, especially when you've your own problems." He slowly let go of Amador's hands. "Speaking of problems, that one has been attended. He leaves tomorrow morning, with orders to be gone before the prayer bell. He is forbidden from ever coming here again, on pain of consequences just short of death. You will not have to worry further upon him."

Amador fought down the need to rail against unasked help. He *needed* help, and it was stupid to keep protesting when that help was offered, no matter what his pride said. "That reminds me: I have a gift for you."

"A gift?" Shock filled Sohan's face, more open, unguarded emotion than Amador had ever seen from him.

Face heating, Amador pulled the gift from his pocket. "It's not much, but I do appreciate all you've done for me, Your Majesty."

"Thank you," Sohan said softly as he accepted, hands lingering on Amador's again, the touch of his warm fingers fading slowly as he withdrew. "I will see you tomorrow, hopefully sooner rather than later, but there's never any telling with my schedule."

Amador smiled. "I understand. Tomorrow then, Your Majesty, and thank you again."

Sohan hesitated, as if he wanted to say something else, but in the end, only nodded and took his leave, bodyguards folding in around him.

"Oh, la la," Marcellette said, making Amador whip around, his face hotter than ever. "I knew our good king was more than a little smitten, but mercy me." She fanned herself hard enough to send the curls around her face fluttering.

"Smitten? With me?" Amador shook his head. "That's absurd."

Vladlena snorted as she refilled her champagne. "You're joking, right? *I* was so clueless about Marci's interest in me that I didn't figure it out until she kissed me, and even I can see that if you asked for the moon His Majesty would obtain it for you. Never seen him act like that. It's positively mind-boggling."

"I think the two of you are simply seeing hearts everywhere," Amador replied, his own stupid heart racing anyway.

Marcellette scoffed, and after Vladlena had refilled all their glasses, lifted hers, "To love and mischief."

Amador smiled as he lifted his own glass. "To love and mischief."

They drank until the champagne and the food were gone, and Amador's head spun so much that he'd probably hate everything when he woke up.

Leaving the glass room, they giggled

and stumbled their way through the halls, assisted by Amador's amused-looking bodyguards.

Once he'd seen Marcellette and Vladlena to their room, Amador shuffled off to his own, head filled with champagne and daydreams. In his room, he waved off Bibiana, who ignored him and with soft snickers helped him get undressed and into bed, where she made him drink a horrid tasting tonic before finally permitting him to sleep.

He woke hours later to someone pounding on his door, though whether it was urgency or excitement, Amador couldn't tell. He dragged his eyes open with a groan as he sat up, but though his head ached, it wasn't nearly as bad as he'd feared it would be. "Who in the world could that be?"

Climbing out of bed, he pulled on a dressing robe just as Bibiana opened the door. A moment later, she opened it wide enough to admit someone, and Nazaire came rushing into the room, eyes sweeping, and brightening as he spotted Amador. "There you are!"

"Here I am?" Amador replied, and yelped as Nazaire swept him up into a tight hug. "Um. Good morning."

Nazaire laughed. "Going on lunch, actually. I am told I have you to thank for locking Léonce in my room last night."

"That didn't take long," Amador said with a smile. "I hope he's not too put out with me."

"No, not even a little bit. Between helping us and helping Marcellette and Vladlena, you've been quite busy. Even Lipovsky is singing your praises, and I don't think I've ever heard him say anything nice about anyone." He hugged Amador again, then shook him gently. "Come, come, you must get dressed! Lots to do today! Including meeting with my brother before he worries and sulks himself to death."

Amador shook his head, laughing as he went to get dressed as told. "I hardly think His Majesty is sulking because of me."

"The lack of you, strictly speaking," Nazaire said, "and he most definitely is."

Shooting Nazaire a disbelieving look, Amador hurried off. He gave Bibiana a look as she pulled out his beautiful sky blue jacket with gray pinstripes and matching gray breeches, paired with boots of a slightly darker gray and glittering diamonds for jewelry. "Seems a bit much for going to lunch."

"Seems perfect for being courted by a king," Bibiana said breezily, finishing off with the perfume that Sohan had given him. "Off with you. Shoo."

Face hot, Amador obediently shooed.

Nazaire brightened to see him, and before Amador could so much as get a word out, was dragging him off through the palace, the bodyguards barely able to keep pace.

As they approached the main hall, though, a group of people crossed their path at an intersecting hallway. Amador went cold as his eyes landed on Ottokar.

Strangely, Ottokar didn't say a word, and it was only then that Amador realized that the men walking on either side of him were *holding* him.

"You're supposed to be gone already," Nazaire said coldly, moving to stand slightly in front of Amador.

Another man, handsome and graying, broke from the crowd. "There was an unavoidable delay, Your Highness. The matter is settled now, though, and I am escorting His Highness home personally. Prince Sanz, I apologize profusely for the way Prince Ottokar has treated you. I've already sent a written report of the matter, and will repeat it in person to Their Majesties upon my arrival. You never should have been treated so, and it will not happen again."

"It had better not," said a new voice, and Amador couldn't help the hot rush of anticipation that swept through him as he registered Sohan's voice. "As we have all crossed paths, I think Prince Amador deserves to hear directly from the source why he was treated so abysmally."

Ottokar said nothing, simply glared hatefully at all of them. One of his eyes was blackened, as though he'd been punched, and there was a cut that spoke to a ring the assailant had worn.

"Fine then," Sohan said, when even the gray-haired man, who must be an ambassador or something, was silent and shame-faced. "Prince Ottokar has a reputation for… mistreating people, shall we say, and that is only the tamest of the scandals he's worked hard to smother. His parents issued an ultimatum: marry you, which would be a strong enough union to forgive the troubles and embarrassment he's caused them, or he would be disowned at the end of this year."

Amador's mouth dropped open. "What?"

"If only he'd learned something instead of simply digging in his heels. Get rid of him."

The men holding Ottokar resumed walking, all but dragging him along with them, the gray-haired man trailing behind a few paces, his face set with deep lines.

Once they were gone, Nazaire released his hold on Amador's arm. "I *was* going to drag you to lunch, so we could sing your praises and demand details of all the stories we've heard, but I believe my brother is about to pull rank, so I'll see you later." He hugged Amador one last time, then headed off down the hall, whistling the whole way.

Leaving Amador and Sohan alone, save for the unassuming bodyguards.

Offering his arm, Sohan smiled and said, "Might I steal a few moments of your time, my prince of the hour?"

"I would be honored," Amador said, twining his own arm through Sohan's, heart in his throat. His bodyguards joined Sohan's, folding in around them smoothly and effortlessly.

Wherever he'd expected to end up, it certainly wasn't in Sohan's private chambers, beautifully appointed in warm browns accented with golds and reds, the scent of leather and silk and amber filling the space. His heart was going to pop any moment.

Sohan poured them wine from a carafe on a table by the open balcony doors and offered him one. "Do you like the perfume, then?" he asked.

"It's lovely," Amador replied as he took the wine, cheeks flushing. Sparkles caught his eyes, and his heart gave another alarming jump as he realized Sohan was wearing his bracelet. He flushed anew as Sohan caught his gaze.

"Thank you," Sohan said. "I rarely receive a gift that isn't perfunctory. The last thank you I received was an ugly vase the servants buried in the hallway leading to the vault."

Amador laughed. "That bad?"

"It's orange and puce. I think they gave it to me just to see what I'd do. Every time I see it, I want to pitch it out a window. I keep hoping a servant will break it, accidentally or 'accidentally'. Alas, the vase stands strong so far." He lifted a hand to wave the words away. "I did not bring you here to discuss ugly vases, though." He took a sip of wine and then set the glass on the table.

Instead of one hand the way Amador had expected, Sohan offered both.

Heart drumming in his ears, drowning out the rest of the world, Amador abandoned his own wine and placed his hands in Sohan's. "You don't have to hold my hand every time you're going to say something important."

"Propriety forbids doing as I'd like," Sohan said, knocking the breath right out of him. "I don't think it's any great secret that you have been traveling the world in search of a spouse."

Amador was going to pass out. "To be perfectly honest, I was traveling the world to avoid my family and Ottokar. Marriage, a new home, would have been a marvelous bonus."

Sohan ran his thumbs over the tops of Amador's hands, the touch soft and warm, somehow reassuring, even as it sent delicate shivers down Amador's spine. "Well, I do not want to get ahead of myself, but you seem to be making a home for yourself here all on your own. Certainly my brother and his coterie will defend you to the death. After all the happiness you've brought, you are welcome here for as long as you desire to remain. That being said, I was hoping you might grant me leave to court you."

"You—" Amador's mouth opened. Closed. Everyone had said it. Everyone had teased him. "Why would *you* want to court *me*?"

"Why in the world would I not? You are beautiful inside and out. You are smart. You work hard. You're generous and kind. However, being courted by a king is quite a different thing than being courted by a fellow prince or princess. There is a great deal more ado, and danger, and responsibility should things progress to the usual end. I would understand if you did not want to take on that burden."

Amador's hands tightened on Sohan's, throat raw as he tried to speak, failing a few times before he finally managed, "I could never consider you, or anything about you, a burden. I would be honored, Your Majesty."

Letting go of one hand, Sohan took the other in both of his and kissed the back of it, lingering just a moment overlong. "Then call me Sohan, please."

"Sohan," Amador repeated softly, and when his hand was released, he succumbed to an overwhelming urge to rest it against the side of Sohan's face, enjoying the warmth and softness of his skin, the brush of his beard. "If I'd known all it took to gain a suitor was to crash into him and topple into a pond, I would have tried it sooner."

Sohan chuckled, and his arms came up slowly to twine around Amador. "I would greatly prefer you not almost-drown yourself to get attention. Or at all. You are, however, welcome to throw yourself into my arms at any time." He leaned down, close enough to nuzzle, to share breath. "I have liked the way you fit in them from the very start."

Gathering every shred of courage he possessed, Amador closed the remaining space between them, pressing his lips to Sohan's. That earned him a pleased noise that shivered right through him, and then he was hauled up, Sohan rising to his full height and taking Amador with him. One of his arms shifted so he could thread his hands through Amador's hair, adjusting him to just the right angle for devouring.

Amador had enjoyed several kisses in his life, a few of them remarkable, but not a one compared to being kissed breathless by

Sohan, held close, possessively, as though he was being marked *property of* in a way that left him moaning, instead of cold with fear as Ottokar had always left him.

When they finally drew apart, Sohan rubbed his thumb over Amador's lips, which did not help Amador regain his thoughts. "The perfume suits you. I hoped it would. I chose the scent with utmost care. Enough I think my perfumier was about to lob something at my head."

Amador laughed. "You did not."

"Oh, I did."

"There was no reason to go to so much trouble," Amador said, still chuckling as Sohan kissed him again.

He reached up reflexively as they drew apart, wrapping his fingers around Sohan's wrist, and was immediately distracted by the feel of the bracelet. "So you like it?"

"Like it? I think— Oh, you mean the bracelet." Sohan grinned, sweet and wicked all at once, melting Amador's brain all over again. "Yes, though I admit I thought at first the color was merely a reference to the pond. It wasn't until one of my chamber servants commented on how perfectly it matched my eyes that I realized there was more to it."

Amador laughed. "Really?"

"Really," Sohan said, looking sheepish. "In my defense, my eyes are rather unremarkable. Everyone in the family but Nazaire has them."

"I disagree vehemently."

How that led to more kisses, Amador didn't quite know, but he certainly wasn't going to complain.

The next time they drew apart, Sohan stepped away entirely and handed Amador's wine back to him. "If I don't stop now, I'll never make the meeting I need to attend in half an hour."

Amador laughed, flushed and pleased. "What meeting is that?"

"The one where Lipovsky officially announces his heir to the council. Nazaire and the others probably meant to tell you at lunch before I stole you away. Speaking of which, it's scarcely been a day, but already Lipovsky has turned into a new person. He has become a doting father, I vow it."

"I'm sure the fact his daughter is marrying into one of the most powerful titles in the kingdom helps with that," Amador replied wryly.

"That and many other things he did not bother to notice until he was forced to. I don't know they'll ever be a happy, cozy family, but I believe there is a strong partnership forming. You have a deft hand."

Amador looked at this wine, twirling the delicate glass in his fingers. "I like to see people happy, especially when I thought I would be marrying Ottokar."

"That will never happen, and if I could punch him again, I would do so happily," Sohan said. "If he ever shows his face—"

"You punched him?" Amador's mouth dropped. "Why?"

"Because he deserved it," Sohan said shortly. "Enough about that cretin. Shall I escort you to lunch before I am dragged back into meetings? Perhaps we can dine privately for dinner?"

"I'd like that," Amador replied as he took Sohan's offered arm.

They walked back through the palace at a leisurely pace, Sohan relating his plans and asking questions regarding dinner, but even focused on the conversation, it was hard to miss the looks and whispers that chased them. "Why is everyone staring so much?"

"Probably because not once in my life have I ever walked so with anyone but my sisters, and that's a very different thing," Sohan replied with a smile.

"Oh," Amador said faintly, half-fearing he'd pass out. "You really want to court *me*?"

Sohan looked at him, those green eyes so intense that Amador was left feeling as though he'd stood too close to a fire and overheated. "Yes, I do. You would make a fine consort, and the rest of the world is stupid if they missed that. However, all I want is you, however I may have you."

"I don't want to be anywhere but here," Amador said, the words barely above a whisper, and he really wished they were still back in Sohan's rooms. He could wait until later, though. Dinner, or after dinner.

As they reached the table where Nazaire, Marcellette, Vladlena, and even Léonce sat, Sohan released him with a kiss to his hand. "Enough," he said when the others immediately started in with cheers and questions. "Do not torment him, you rapscallions. Do not let the court torment him either. Nazaire, I'm entrusting the matter to you whenever I'm not present."

Nazaire snorted. "You may as well appoint Marcellette. She's the one the court is terrified of, not me."

"Where goeth one troublemaker, so goeth all," Sohan drawled. "At least *pretend* to behave. I'll see you all later."

He left, immediately enfolded by various nobles, and Amador took his seat as the others grinned shamelessly at him. "What?"

"Soo…." Marcellette asked. "Were we right? Were we right? That outfit says we were, as does the way your hair—"

"Stop it," Vladlena said idly, rolling her eyes at Marcellette's pout.

"What's wrong with my hair?" Amador hissed frantically as he tried to smooth it back into place, which set all of them to laughing.

Nazaire grinned. "The court is having kittens, you know. At least two thirds of them have been trying to woo, or outright seduce, my brother and gained exactly nothing for their efforts. You're here not even two weeks and you've been spotted walking arm-in-arm with him. They are having *fits*. It's *delightful*."

Léonce gave him a look. "Stop being a brat."

"Not a chance," Nazaire replied. "Just wait until I write to my siblings. We're going to be merciless. Sohan's had this coming for a long time."

Amador huffed. "Is this what our entire courtship is going to be like?"

"Yes," Nazaire and Marcellette replied, as Vladlena and Léonce rolled their eyes.

Sighing in defeat, Amador poured himself some wine and submitted to the torrent of questions and teasing remarks, and unsubtle interruptions from nosy courtiers looking for gossip.

It was more attention than he'd ever had in his life, and more than a little disconcerting. Also fun, though, to not be tucked away on the sidelines, watching and helping, but never really *there*. Not like this. Not like he was part of the group. Part of the family. Even his own kin didn't treat him this way.

Besides, he'd have to get used to it. He'd traveled the world in search of a prince or princess to court, and not once ever imagined he'd instead wind up courted by a king. Consort was a very different role than prince, and Amador would travel the world thrice over if that was what it took to remain at Sohan's side forever.

Thankfully, it seemed like all he really had to do was stay right where he was.

About the Author

Megan is a long-time resident of queer romance and keeps herself busy reading and writing it. She is often accused of fluff and nonsense. When she's not involved in writing, she likes to cook, harass her wife and cats, or watch movies. She loves to hear from readers and can be found all over the internet.

meganderr.com
patreon.com/meganderr
meganderr.blogspot.com
facebook.com/meganaprilderr
meganaderr@gmail.com
@meganaderr